HOME TEAM

Eric Walters,
Jerome "Junk Yard Dog" Williams
and Johnnie Williams III

ORCA BOOK PUBLISHERS

Library and Archives Canada Cataloguing in Publication

Walters, Eric, 1957-
Home team / written by Eric Walters, Jerome Williams and Johnnie Williams III.

(Orca young readers)
ISBN 978-1-55469-218-7

I. Williams, Jerome, 1973-   II. Williams, Johnnie, III III. Title.
IV. Series: Orca young readers
PS8595.A598H64 2010   jC813'.54   C2009-907251-3

First published in the United States, 2010
Library of Congress Control Number: 2009940901

Summary: Against all odds, Nick and Kia set out to persuade the Toronto Raptors'
community relations department to send players to visit their school.

Mixed Sources
Cert no. SW-COC-001271
© 1996 FSC
FSC

*Orca Book Publishers is dedicated to preserving the environment and has printed this book
on paper certified by the Forest Stewardship Council.*

Orca Book Publishers gratefully acknowledges the support for its publishing programs
provided by the following agencies: the Government of Canada through the Canada Book Fund
and the Canada Council for the Arts, and the Province of British Columbia through the
BC Arts Council and the Book Publishing Tax Credit.

Cover design by Teresa Bubela
Front cover photograph (top) by Laura Leyshon
Front cover photograph (bottom) by Getty Images

ORCA BOOK PUBLISHERS   ORCA BOOK PUBLISHERS
PO Box 5626, STN. B   PO Box 468
VICTORIA, BC CANADA   CUSTER, WA USA
V8R 6S4   98240-0468

www.orcabook.com
Printed and bound in Canada.
13 12 11 10 • 4 3 2 1

To the members of my Home Team—my great friends Johnnie and Jerome and the hundreds and hundreds of members of the Toronto District School Board reading clubs who made this the book what it is. It's an honor to be part of such an incredible team!

Eric Walters

To all the Read To Succeed participants who love reading and basketball. As a former professional athlete and current Global Ambassador, I can assure you that the NBA CARES about young readers. So inflate your mind and bounce towards your dreams.

Jerome "JYD" Williams

To my Lailah Buggins, who is just beginning her educational journey. I would like for her to always remember that literacy will help her navigate towards her dreams. So read to succeed.

Johnnie Williams III

Chapter One

"And just before we start our assignment," Mrs. Orr said, "can somebody, once more, just to be certain we all understand, tell us the difference between a *friendly* letter and a *business* letter?"

A flock of hands went up. I knew the answer, but there was no point in being a show-off about it.

"Jennifer," Mrs. Orr said.

"A friendly letter is written to a friend and a business letter is written to a business," she answered, stating the obvious.

"That is correct," Mrs. Orr said.

Jennifer gave a smug little smile, like she'd just invented a car that ran on water instead of giving the world's lamest answer. My problem was I hated lame. I hated obvious. And I hated suck-ups. This was grade six—maybe only the first week of grade six, but still it *was* grade six. Shouldn't we be old enough to avoid all of that?

I stuck up my hand.

"Yes, Nicholas?" Mrs. Orr asked.

"What if your friend is running the business that you're writing to? Is that a friendly letter to a business or a business letter to a friend?"

There was a twittering of giggles. That only encouraged me.

"Or what if it is your friend, but you want to write something that is businessy...is that a word? Well, either way, is that a friendly letter or—?"

"It *isn't* a word," she said, cutting me off. "And it isn't who you're writing to, but the *nature* of the letter."

"Okay, now you've got me confused," I said. I turned to the class. "Am I alone here?"

Kia's hand went up immediately, followed by hand after hand until more than half the class had a hand in the air. I didn't know if Kia was really confused, but it was guaranteed she'd back me up on it regardless. After all, she was my best friend.

"Since many people seem less than clear, it's probably a good idea for us to clarify it further then," Mrs. Orr said. "Thank you for bringing that up, Nicholas."

"You're...um...welcome," I stammered. I wasn't trying to be helpful—I was trying to be difficult or funny or something.

"For example, Nicholas, to whom did you write your friendly letter? Oh, wait, I remember...it was some basketball player. I can't quite recall his name."

"Wayne Dawkins," I said, unable to believe that she couldn't remember *his* name. "And he isn't *some* basketball player, he's *the* star of the Raptors."

"My apologies," she said. "When you wrote your friendly letter to him, what were you saying?"

"I was just telling him how much I like watching him play and how good I think he is. And telling him what I like to do, who I am. That sort of thing."

"So the tone of the letter was friendly, like you were writing to a friend."

"I *wish* he was my friend."

3

Actually I *did* have a friend who had been in the NBA. My buddy, Jerome "JYD" Williams. JYD were the initials for Junk Yard Dog, a nickname he got because he played the game with such intensity. Before he retired he'd played with four different teams—Detroit, Chicago, New York and, of course, Toronto.

"The letter we're going to be writing today," Mrs. Orr said, "is not about friendly things but is directed toward getting something, making a complaint, offering a compliment or requesting something."

"Could I write to Wayne Dawkins and request that he become my friend?" I asked.

The whole class broke out in laughter.

"I'm afraid not. There has to be a more specific business request—as I said, a compliment or a complaint or a suggestion."

"Couldn't I compliment him on his play, or complain about the referees, or suggest that they win more or complain that he's not my friend?"

More laughter, which Mrs. Orr silenced with a glare. This was only the second week of school, but a lot of us had had Mrs. Orr as our grade-three teacher, and we knew not to mess with her. She was fair, and I liked her, but she was pretty strict.

"Just to be clear, Nick, you cannot—I repeat—*cannot* write to Wayne Dawkins," she said. "You have to write to a business to make a business request." She paused. "Understood?"

"Understood," I mumbled.

The door opened and Mr. Roberts, our gym teacher, walked in. He was dressed, as always, in his sweats, a school T-shirt and big red basketball shoes. I didn't know what size those shoes were, but if they were a couple of sizes bigger, he could have swapped footwear with Ronald McDonald. Not that I was making fun of him, but just saying...He was a pretty cool teacher and they *were* great basketball shoes. Just a little big. Well, unless you were a clown.

"Now that we all understand our assignment, I'll leave the class in the capable hands of Mr. Roberts."

I wanted to hoot, but I knew better. Bigfoot wasn't just our gym teacher but also the coach of all the school teams, including my favorite— the basketball team. Our season was just about

to start, and I was really looking forward to it...
well, mostly.

"So what's the assignment today, boss?" he
asked Mrs. Orr.

"They're working on business letters. If you
can help them with their writing assignment,
that would be wonderful," Mrs. Orr told him.

"No problem. Letters...I know all twenty-six of
them...from *A* to *Z*."

Mrs. Orr gave him a questioning look and then
smiled. She knew he was joking. He was always
joking. Except during basketball games—then
he was dead serious.

Mrs. Orr gathered up her marking and other
things she'd need from the desk. She stopped
at the door.

"It's important that they get a good start on
these," she suggested.

He gave her a little salute, and she left and
closed the door behind her.

Three times a week Mr. Roberts came into the
class to supervise and teach us when Mrs. Orr
had planning time. I really looked forward to
those times. Not that I didn't like Mrs. Orr—
she was my favorite regular teacher of all time,

even if she was kind of strict—but Mr. Roberts was more fun. So much fun that he would often get sidetracked and forget to have us do the work we were supposed to do. That's why he always got a little extra warning and a side look from Mrs. Orr.

He walked around the room as we all started thinking or working on our letters. That was how he spent almost the whole time in our class—patrolling. The rare time he sat down at Mrs. Orr's desk, he did more bouncing than sitting. He was constantly tapping his foot or fumbling with his hands or munching on some snack food or drinking from his water bottle. He had a lot of trouble sitting still. I think he was kind of hyper. Yeah, he definitely was. Maybe hyperactive boys grew up to be gym teachers with big feet. That wouldn't be a bad job. Maybe I should become a gym teacher—well, at least after my career in the NBA was over.

I noticed that hardly anybody was actually writing. They were all sitting there, pen in hand, thinking. Or at least pretending to think. Obviously this wasn't an easy letter to write. Certainly not as easy as the friendly letter.

I guess we all had friends, but how many kids in grade six had a business they wanted to write to? We were eleven and twelve years old. What did we have to do with any businesses?

"Hey, Nick," Mr. Roberts said as he bounced over beside my desk. "Did you catch the game last night?"

"Yeah, like he'd miss a Raptors game," Kia said before I could answer.

He turned to Kia. "Look who's talking. When was the last time you missed a game?"

"Well...I missed a few...before I was born."

"So what did *you* think of last night's game?"

"It was good...until the end," Kia said.

"That game drove me crazy!" I exclaimed. "Leading by three points with five seconds left and they didn't foul anybody! Don't they under-stand basketball at all?"

"Exactly!" Mr. Roberts agreed. "Basketball 101 states that you should foul the guy and put him on the line. Then, even if he gets both free throws, you're still leading by one point and you get back the ball and the game is over."

"Instead they sink a three-pointer, tie the game and we lose in overtime. I wanted to kick the TV," I said.

"Yeah, I was so frustrated that—" Mr. Roberts stopped. "Maybe we should stop talking about basketball and you should get back to work. I don't want either of us to get in trouble. You better finish your letters."

"I will finish...but first I better start," I said.

"You haven't started?"

I held up the blank sheet. "Not yet. This isn't easy."

"You had no problem with the last letter," he said.

"That was to Wayne Dawkins."

"Speaking of Wayne Dawkins, my friend John teaches at a school in the city and he told me that they had a special guest visit their school last week." He paused. "Wayne Dawkins."

"Wayne Dawkins came to their school?" I gasped.

He nodded his head. "He spoke at an assembly for the whole school."

"But...but...why? How...how did that happen?"

"Apparently the Raptors schedule community visits to schools to promote reading."

"We're a school," I said. "We need to be told to read...we're in the community. Can we get him to come to our school?"

"I don't see why not."

"So how do we get him to come?" I demanded.

He pushed the piece of paper on my desk toward me. "Maybe you should write a letter."

"But Mrs. Orr said I *can't* write to Wayne Dawkins."

"Not to him. Write to the Raptors' community relations director."

"The Raptors...Wait...they're a business," I replied.

"A big business."

"So if I write a letter to the Raptors and ask for Wayne Dawkins to come to our school, then I'm actually doing the assignment, right?" I asked. "I'm writing a business letter."

"Well, it sounds right to me."

"That's incredible. I finish an assignment and get to meet Wayne Dawkins."

"Slow down there," Mr. Roberts said. "Finishing the assignment part is guaranteed. Getting Wayne Dawkins probably won't happen."

"But why not?"

"My guess is they get hundreds, maybe thousands, of requests like that, so your letter might just get lost, like a needle in a haystack of letters," Mr. Roberts explained.

What he was saying did make sense Unfortunately.

"What about two needles?" Kia asked. "I could write a letter as well."

"Two letters should double your chances for sure," Mr. Roberts agreed.

"Then three would triple our chances, right?" Greg asked.

"Definitely. The more the better."

"Wait," I said as I jumped to my feet. "Everybody, wait!"

The whole class was looking at me standing there. I had an idea. It was either an incredible idea or an incredibly *stupid* idea. But fifty-fifty odds weren't bad.

Slowly I looked around the room. Everybody was staring at me, waiting. Lailah was looking at me too. Was she smiling—or was that a smirk? Either way, she *was* looking at me.

Lailah was new to the school this year. I had a clear memory of her being walked into our class by the principal, Mr. Waldman, on the second day of school. She had really nice clothes—she always dressed well—and she came in really confidently. I'd seen new kids walk in before, and it always looked like they were on their way to the dentist. Not her. She walked in like she owned the place and—

"Okay, we're waiting," Kia said.

"Oh yeah, sure." I took a deep breath. "I *think* we all should write a letter to the Raptors."

There was a mumbling of agreement and nodding of heads. "If we all write, we should have twenty-five times the chance of getting Wayne Dawkins to visit our school, or maybe another player from the team."

"The more the better," Mr. Roberts said. "They'd see that it's a whole class that wants this to happen."

"We can't do that," Ashley said sharply.

"Why not?" Mr. Roberts and I asked in unison.

"Well...it wasn't what Mrs. Orr assigned."

"She didn't say we couldn't all write a letter to the same business," I said. "Did anybody hear her say that?"

"No...but...I don't *want* to write to the Raptors. I've already started my letter." She held up her paper. There were a few lines written.

"No one *has* to write to the Raptors," Mr. Roberts said.

"Good, because I'm writing to my father's

business," Ashley said.

How typical and annoying. That was her—typically annoying. If I were her father, I wouldn't write back if she wrote to me.

"*I'm* going to write to the Raptors," Lailah said. She gave me a big smile.

"Me too," another kid added from the back.

"By a show of hands, how many are going to write to the Raptors?" Mr. Roberts asked.

Hand after hand went up. I did a quick count—twenty-two out of twenty-five. That gave us twenty-two times the power of just a letter from me...well, I knew Kia would have written the Raptors too, so we would have at least eleven times the power.

"Good," Mr. Roberts said. "You all get writing, and I'll get an address and contact person to address the letters to."

Mr. Roberts went over and plopped himself down in front of a computer. Everybody else began talking. There was a real buzz in the room. A buzz was good, as long as I didn't get stung.

I got up and went over to stand beside Mr. Roberts. I had a question—a question triggered by Ashley. She was annoying but she was also really smart—come to think of it, that was part of what made her so annoying.

Mr. Roberts turned from the computer to look at me.

"I was just wondering if—"

"If Mrs. Orr is going to be mad about this?" he asked, finishing my sentence.

"Yeah."

"As far as I can tell, you all just followed the assignment. And if she does get angry, she'll be angry at me and not you or anybody else."

"But I don't want to get you in trouble."

"I think I can handle the heat if there is any," he said and chuckled to himself. "But don't worry. I've always believed it's better to ask for forgiveness than permission."

"What?"

"Sometimes I just do what I think is right, and if somebody gets mad at me, then I just tell them I'm sorry."

"Okay, I guess that makes sense."

"It's got me through school and work, and it keeps my marriage working well. Remember this for the future: the most important phrase you can ever say to your wife or girlfriend is—"

"I don't have a girlfriend!" I protested.

"Or a wife either, I hope. But remember, simply saying 'I'm sorry. You were right' can get you out of a lot of trouble."

"I'll try to remember that."

"Good, because you never know when that moment might arrive for you."

He turned around and it looked like he was looking at Lailah! He couldn't mean...I just hoped it wasn't that obvious.

I ran a hand through my hair, trying to smooth it out. Why did it have to be so wild and... brownish? Darker or lighter would have been better. Even if my hair wasn't right, I was in a nice shirt—a nice clean shirt—and I was almost the tallest person in the class. I *was* the tallest if you didn't count Jennifer and Amelia, but I was definitely the tallest boy. Tall was good... although giraffes were tall, and that didn't make them good-looking. But my mother always told me how handsome I was. Then again, what mother didn't think her kid was good-looking? And who really cared if their mother thought they were handsome? I *did* know my eyes were nice. Nice and blue and—

"You know, Nick, the very best guarantee that Mrs. Orr won't be upset is if the letters are both finished and well-written...finished before she gets back. You better stop daydreaming and get writing, buddy."

Chapter Two

Dear Ms. Allison,

I am writing on behalf of me and my school. We are all big basketball fans. We are particularly big Raptors fans and even bigger fans of Wayne Dawkins. I think he is a superstar. I was told that sometimes NBA players come to schools for a visit. We are a school and we would like him to come to visit. He wouldn't have to stay long and he wouldn't have to shoot hoops with us or anything—but we'd let him if he wanted to. We have a nice gym.

If he came on a Tuesday—any Tuesday— it is pizza day and he could have some pizza. It would be free for him. He could have as many slices as he wanted.

You can write us back at the address listed below or even call the number that is there to arrange to come to our school.

Thank you.

Sincerely,

Nick

P.S. You might have noticed that there are 22 letters from my class. We're not asking for him to come to the school 22 times. Once would be good enough.

Chapter Three

"Okay, everybody!" Mr. Roberts yelled.

We all stopped and held on to the balls, leaving the gym in silence.

"I'm not going to say that was the worst practice in the history of basketball." He paused. "Because I haven't seen *every* practice in the history of basketball...but that was not very good. Although we are getting better each practice, and we *will* continue to get better, because as you all know, a winner doesn't quit..."

"...and a quitter doesn't win!" we all yelled back.

Mr. Roberts had lots of sayings and we knew them all.

"Let's get back to practice!" he called out. "Layup drill!"

We got back into the two lines. One line went in for the layups and the other line got the rebound. I was tired of layup drills. I was tired of practicing the basketball basics over and over again, doing things that most of our team just didn't seem to get.

Our school team had always been good, but this season was probably going to be a long one. Aside from Kia and me, there really wasn't anybody. Most of the team had graduated and gone on to the middle school for grade seven. And then the twins, Brad and Brent, moved away, and Greg got hurt on the playground and wasn't able to play.

Greg's injury was just so stupid. We were playing some basketball at recess and he'd tripped on one of the little kids and sprained his ankle so badly that he couldn't play for weeks.

Greg's injury was bad, but the reason for his injury was also hurting us. Normally we could play basketball during lunch and recess, but that wasn't so easy right now. The field was being repaired—it was being levelled and new sod put down, and the baseball diamond was being replaced. That was all good. But in the meantime nobody was allowed on the field, which meant that everyone had to stay on the pavement and the basketball court was flooded with kids.

Mr. Roberts blew his whistle and we all stopped. He looked like he was trying to figure out what to say next. I knew what I would have said to a bunch of kids who couldn't make layups, but I knew he wouldn't say that.

"The morning bell is just about to go. Thank you all for coming out, and remember, you only fail when you fail to try. I'll see you all right after school, right here in the gym, for our first game of the season."

There was a mumble of excitement. I *wasn't* excited. I was smart enough to know we should all be pretty scared about what was going to happen.

"Now, head off to class and no fooling around in the hall."

Everybody went to the change room except for Kia and me. We always stayed to help put away the balls—part of our responsibilities as co-captains of the team.

"So," Mr. Roberts said, "what do you two think of the team?"

Kia and I exchanged a look. Did he want an honest answer?

"Um...we'll win some games this year," I said.

"That's a very polite answer from one of my co-captains. Kia, in a couple of words, how would you describe our team?"

"We suck."

He laughed. "That certainly is a couple of words."

"Actually, *we* don't suck," she said, pointing first to me and then to herself, "but the rest of the team is seriously challenged."

"Nick, do you agree? Do you think the team is challenged?"

Reluctantly I nodded my head.

"Do either of you think we have any chance of defending our title and winning it all again this year?" he asked.

"There's always a chance," I said.

"There's a chance I'm going to learn to fly, but I think it's probably a pretty small chance," Kia added.

He nodded his head ever so slightly in agreement. "I guess you two know what that means, right?"

For a split second I thought "quit," but I knew that wasn't the answer he was looking for.

"We have to try to work as hard as we can, game by game, starting with tonight's game, hoping that we get better," I said.

"We will get better when Greg can play again," Kia added.

"We will, but that won't be tonight. And who knows? Maybe we can convince Wayne Dawkins to suit up for the team for one of our games when he comes to visit the school. The letters did go out, right?" asked Mr. Roberts.

"Mrs. Orr mailed them a couple of weeks ago," I said.

First she'd photocopied and marked them all. I got a level four. So did Kia.

When she first found out that most of us were sending letters to the same place, she seemed a bit angry. No, that wasn't right—she seemed very annoyed. I started to explain why Mr. Roberts said it was okay, and then I remembered what he had said to me. I told her I was sorry if we did it wrong and it was *all* my fault. Amazingly, after that she seemed okay with everything. It worked! I still didn't know how it would work with a girlfriend or wife, but it seemed to work pretty well with teachers.

"With or without Wayne Dawkins, we'll get by," Mr. Roberts said. "We're just lucky to have two co-captains who aren't going to quit or let anybody else quit."

"Right."

"No matter how bad it gets," he added.

"How bad could it get?" I asked.

He didn't answer except to shrug his shoulders—which was, I guess, an answer. I knew we were going to find out, starting with tonight's game.

I stood and sang along with the national anthem. I turned ever so slightly so I could see Lailah but nobody could see that I was looking at her.

She was wearing another new outfit. She seemed to be in something different every day. Wow...that was scary. Not that she had that many clothes but that *I* noticed them. I actually *knew* her clothing. Worse still, I knew which of her clothes I liked. Either I was starting to like girls or I was becoming one.

Lailah looked my way and smiled. I quickly looked away. The anthem ended and I slumped into my seat, glad to be out of her sight.

The announcements followed. There were the usual ones—including a reminder to stay off the field and to be careful of the equipment the men were using to fix it. The final announcement got my attention.

"And we wish our Clark Boulevard Cougars good luck tonight in their first game of the season," our principal, Mr. Waldman, said.

A little cheer came from our class and an echo from other classes down the hall.

"We hope for another undefeated season. Go Clark Cougars!"

The cheering was even louder. Oh great, just what we needed was to raise the expectations. The way we were playing, the only time we'd be undefeated was before tonight's game started. I'd have to enjoy that until then because we weren't going to enjoy much about this season.

"Okay, let's get to work," Mrs. Orr said.

She wasn't wasting any time at all this morning.

"I'm happy to say that we received our first reply from our business letters," she said.

For a split second I got excited, thinking it was the Raptors, but then I remembered that Ashley had written to her father. I had to figure that even if he did find her as annoying as the rest of us, he'd still write her back, and fast.

"Or more accurately," Mrs. Orr said, "we received a reply to twenty-two of your letters."

"The Raptors wrote back!" I exclaimed, practically jumping out of my seat.

Everybody started to cheer, and Mrs. Orr silenced everybody by raising her hand slightly.

"What does it say?" Kia asked.

"Nick, since you started all of this, why don't you read the letter to the class," Mrs. Orr said.

I jumped to my feet. Normally reading out loud in front of the class would rank pretty low on my priority list, but not reading this letter.

You could have heard a pin drop as I took the letter from Mrs. Orr. Right up on the top of the page was a big Raptors emblem—official Raptors paper. Pretty darn classy. I cleared my throat and then took a deep breath.

"'Dear Clark Boulevard Students,'" I read. "'Thank you so much for your letters to our organization. It sounds like Clark has some big Raptors fans and wonderful students.'"

There was another cheer from the class. I cleared my throat to silence everybody.

"'Because you are such big Raptors fans, we wanted to respond to you as soon as possible. Thank you very much for your kind invitation for Wayne Dawkins and the rest of the Raptors to come to your school. It was particularly kind of you to offer them a pizza lunch—pizza is Wayne's favorite food.'"

I looked at Kia and we exchanged smiles. We both knew that already—which was why we'd both mentioned that in our letters to the Raptors. I went back to the letter.

"'And since you are all such big fans I know you'll understand when I tell you that unfortunately Wayne has to decline your offer—'"

I stopped reading and looked at Mrs. Orr. "Declined...as in he's not coming?"

"It doesn't look like it."

"Are *any* of the Raptors coming?" I asked.

"Please continue reading," she said.

I didn't want to read anything anymore, but what choice did I have?

"'Every year we receive literally hundreds of visit requests from individuals, schools and community organizations. Unfortunately the players can't make all those visits and still have time to practice and play basketball, so we are not able to send a player to your school this year.'"

We were getting nobody. Not even the twelfth guy who just sat on the bench. Nobody.

"Finish the letter, please, Nick."

I didn't want to finish the letter. I just wanted to slip away away where nobody would be looking at me, but I knew finishing the letter was my only way out. There were just a couple more lines.

"'We know you're all great Raptors fans and will continue to support the team. Sincerely, Christina Allison, Director of Community and Public Relations.'"

I slinked back to my desk, eyes down, not wanting to look at anybody. I felt awful. It was the sort of feeling you get when you miss a free throw—an important free throw—and every eye in the gym is on you.

I was still holding the letter. I wanted to ball it up and throw it in the garbage can—but I'd probably miss. Besides, I couldn't do that. I slipped it into my binder, where I wouldn't have to see it.

"Thank you for reading the letter, Nick," Mrs. Orr said. "And that certainly was a successful letter."

"Did I miss something?" Kia asked. "Just how was that successful?"

I wanted to know the answer to that question myself. Probably everybody in the class wanted to hear what she was going to say.

"While no Raptor is going to come to the school, that doesn't mean that your letters were unsuccessful," Mrs. Orr said.

"But how *was* it successful?" Kia asked again.

"The business received your letter, understood your request and replied to your request."

"But they said no," I said.

"They did say no, but they did reply, and that's the thing that made your letters successful."

I guess anything could be a success if you aimed low enough, and this was pretty well as low as you could aim.

Chapter Four

Practice was light and fun, and everybody seemed happy. A win could have that effect. We'd won our game by one point. It was a last-minute shot by me. A lucky, desperate shot that had no right to go in but did. Everybody on the team had celebrated like we'd won the championship instead of beating a team that was almost as bad as us. It wasn't like either team was really good enough to win, but we couldn't *both* lose. Still, it was better to beat a bad team than lose to one.

I put up a shot and it missed everything, even the netting. Major air ball. I just hoped nobody had—

"Glad you didn't do that in the game yesterday," Kia suggested.

Obviously one pair of eyes saw me miss.

"We both had a pretty good game."

"We both had a *great* game," she said quietly. She leaned in even closer. "Which is the *only* reason we won."

"Yeah, I guess we'll just have to play that way every game and we'll—"

"Still lose most of our games."

"What?"

She pulled me into the corner away from everybody.

"Do you really think that was a good team we beat?" she asked.

"No, of course not. They were bad."

"And we still almost lost to them. Unless we hope that every team is terrible, we're in trouble."

"We're getting better with each practice," I suggested.

"We're getting better because we were so bad we had no place to go but up."

"You two decided to take a mid-practice break?" Mr. Roberts asked as he came up behind us.

"We were just talking...talking strategy," Kia lied.

"And what did you come up with?"

Oh good, let's tell him that our strategy is that we hope all the other teams play worse than we do.

"We were thinking it would be good to spread the points around more," Kia said.

Thank goodness she could always come up with something to say.

"You two scored forty-seven of our fifty-four points," Mr. Roberts said.

"Yeah," Kia agreed. "So we need to feed the other players more."

"I was thinking the opposite," Mr. Roberts said.

"What?" I asked.

"The rest of the team got seven points on twenty-four shots. They hit around eighteen percent of their shots. We can't afford to have them shoot very much. We won because you two played hard, shot well and didn't let the others give up."

"They did *try* hard," Kia agreed.

"They *did*. Think about that last basket," Mr. Roberts said. "The game was basically over, and we could've lost, but Devon goes after that ball, strips it from their player. Then Bilaal practically *kills* himself by grabbing the ball as it goes out of bounds and taps it back in to you, Kia, before he crashes into those seats. And, of course, Kia gets it to you, Nick, and you shoot. But really, if any of those plays weren't made, we would have lost."

Strange. I hadn't thought of any of that, but Mr. Roberts was right.

"We'll just have to keep trying as hard as we can every play of every game," Mr. Roberts said.

"We'll keep hustling," I confirmed.

"I hope so. It's going to be harder once we start losing," he said.

Kia and I looked at each other and then at him. Neither of us was expecting him to say that.

"Come on, you two aren't the only ones who know basketball. For us to have any chance in any game, we'll have to out-hustle everybody. If we don't bring more energy than the other team, we have no chance. It's easier to hustle when you're winning or the game is close. Much harder if you're losing, especially by a lot...and that could happen."

"You better tell them," Kia said, gesturing to the rest of the team. "After yesterday they think we're going to go undefeated."

"It's better if they don't know. Let's not talk to them about any of this. Let them believe, because that may be the best weapon we have." He paused. "Besides, it isn't just about winning."

"It isn't?" Kia questioned.

He shrugged. "Well, winning is nice, but maybe this year winning isn't about the score at the end but how we play the game."

I was pretty sure that winning was based solely on the score at the end of the game, but I didn't think that was what he meant or wanted to hear.

"If we keep on trying, keep on improving, then that will be like a victory," he continued.

Maybe *like* a victory, but certainly *not* a victory.

"And that's why I need the two of you to promise me you will not give up on them and will keep the team from giving up," he said.

"That's a promise," Kia said. "You won't see any quit in either of us."

"No way we'll quit," I agreed.

"No matter how bad it gets, we'll keep a positive attitude. But it sure would have been a real morale booster if the Raptors had agreed to send a player to our school. But there's no chance of that, right?" he asked.

"Their letter was pretty clear that they can't come this year," I said. "The letter said they get hundreds and hundreds of requests and can't say yes to them all."

"Well, I guess they have a point," Mr. Roberts said. "Although sometimes taking no for an answer is too easy."

"What do you mean?" I asked.

"You truly fail when you stop trying to succeed," he said.

"Do you have an idea?" I asked—hoping he did.

"I just *gave* you an idea. Maybe you shouldn't give up so easily," he said.

⚾ ⚾ ⚾

I dribbled a few steps and then skidded to a stop as a little grade-one kid scampered in front of me, chasing a ball. He didn't even notice me. It was lucky I saw him or there could have been another playground collision.

"He's right, you know," Kia said.

"That little kid with the ball?"

"No. Mr. Roberts. He's right. We shouldn't just give up on the idea of having the Raptors come to our school."

"Okay, do you have any bright ideas?"

"Not yet, but—"

"Hi, Nick." It was Lailah. "You played a good game yesterday."

"How would you know?" Kia questioned. "You weren't there."

"Some people listen to the morning announcements. Anyway, I heard he scored twenty-four points."

"There's more to a good game than points," Kia said.

"You mean he didn't play a good game?" Lailah asked.

"Of course he played a good game, but there is more than just how many points somebody gets."

"You mean like his number of rebounds and assists, or maybe he had a lot of steals and played some good D?" Lailah asked.

Kia looked surprised.

"You shouldn't look so shocked," Lailah said to Kia. "You don't have to wear a jersey every day or smell like sweat to know basketball."

Kia was wearing a school jersey but it wasn't sweaty.

"I guess I'm just proud to be part of the team," Kia said, "but you wouldn't know about that."

"I've been on winning teams before."

"With *those* nails?" Kia asked.

Lailah didn't answer but she looked annoyed—very annoyed. Kia was being rude, but she did have a point. It would be hard to play any sport with nails that long.

"Kia got twenty-three points," I said. "She was the second-highest scorer."

"Well, good for her," Lailah said. The tone of her voice certainly didn't match the words.

More silence. Overhead a plane came in, breaking the silence with the noise of its engines. Our school was under one of the flight paths to the airport and on some days, depending on the direction the wind was blowing, we could have planes overhead every few minutes.

The noise faded as the plane passed out of sight.

"They're awfully loud," Lailah said.

"I hardly notice them," I said.

"Me neither," Kia agreed. "But we've gone to this school our whole lives."

Lailah was still so new at the school that she hadn't gotten used to it.

"I never hear them when we're inside the school," Lailah said.

"It's specially built to be soundproof," I added.

"I guess that's why. I was sad about the Raptors not coming," Lailah said.

I really didn't want to talk about this.

"We haven't given up yet," Kia said.

"You haven't?"

"Nope, not quitting."

"So what's the new plan?" Lailah asked, looking right at me for an answer.

"Umm...we don't have anything specific yet."

"But we'll come up with something," Kia said.

"It would be awesome to have them come to the school," Lailah said. "Is there anything I can do to help you?"

"We've got it covered," Kia said, cutting her off. "We don't need any help."

Lailah gave Kia an evil eye and then turned to me, flashed a big smile and walked away.

"I really don't like her," Kia snapped.

"I don't think she's too crazy about you either."

"Good. Now forget about her. Let's try to figure out what we're going to do about the Raptors."

"I thought you had an idea."

"I just said that to get rid of her, but we'll come up with something. Maybe we can write them again."

"That didn't work once so I don't think a second time will help. You don't have any other ideas?" I asked.

She shook her head. "The day is still young."

Chapter Five

We filed into class and took our seats behind the computers. They were high-tech, top-of-the-line and brand-new. They had been funded by the parents' association—my mother was the president. The only thing that wasn't brand-new and high-tech in our computer room was our teacher, Mrs. Carson.

To be fair, she wasn't a computer teacher. She was the music teacher at our school. She just didn't know much about computers. Just like Mr. Roberts did for Mrs. Orr, Mrs. Carson gave the regular computer teacher, Ms. Brown, planning time. Ms. Brown taught every grade in the school except ours. I guess that made some sense. We were the oldest kids, so we already knew lots about computers. Certainly more than Mrs. Carson would ever know.

She *was* a great music teacher though. She played the piano, the guitar and the trumpet. She had a wonderful singing voice. She directed the school play and even wrote songs for it. She was the director of the choir. Unfortunately none of those skills had anything to do with computers. The only keyboard she cared about was on her piano.

"Good afternoon, class," Mrs. Carson said. "Today we are going to be...going to be..."

She looked down at the lesson plan Ms. Brown had left her. It was sad that somebody who could perform so well with music was so helpless in this class.

"Oh, yes, we're going to be learning about sending emails."

There was a groan from the class.

"I know that most of you have probably sent an email or two in your life, but Ms. Brown has left me with a very detailed lesson plan on the *correct* format for emails."

Great. In one class we had to write letters, and in this one we had to email—wait!

I grabbed my binder and flipped through the pages until I found the reply from the Raptors. I'd wanted to throw it out, but I'd kept it—after all, it was from the Raptors. I ran my finger down the page, looking for something...there it was.

Mrs. Carson continued to read from the lesson plan. Nobody was paying any attention. Maybe if she sang the instructions that would have worked.

"Are there any questions?" she asked.

I got the feeling she was really, really hoping nobody would have any questions, and then she wouldn't have to try to give an answer to a question she didn't even understand.

"In that case, everybody should get to work on their email," she said.

She sat down at the desk and I got up. I walked to the front board, carrying the letter with me. I picked up a piece of chalk and in big letters started to print out an email address.

"Nick?" Mrs. Carson asked.

"I'm just writing down an email address...you know...for the assignment."

"Oh, that's good," she said.

I finished writing out the address.

"For anybody who's interested," I said, "this is the email address for the lady at the Raptors who turned down our first request to have a Raptor come to our school."

"We should email her and tell her she's a jerk," Greg said.

"No!" I exclaimed. "I thought that maybe we could email her and ask her again to have somebody come. We could tell her that the invitation is still on."

"That is a great idea," Kia said. "And if everybody emails her, then maybe she'll rethink the whole thing."

"Everybody wrote letters and look how much good *that* did," Ashley chimed in.

"Not *all* of us," Kia said pointedly.

"Do you really think *my* letter would have made that big a difference?" Ashley asked.

"Twenty-six would have been better than twenty-two," Kia snapped.

"But not as good as seventy or eighty," Lailah added.

She stood up and everybody looked at her. She looked so confident. Funny—the way she was standing there so calmly reminded me of the way Kia stood on the line waiting to take a free throw.

"You can't seriously think that we should all write *three* emails," Ashley said.

"No. I was thinking that we could have everybody in the three grade-six classes send her an email," Lailah replied.

"That's right. Mrs. Carson, you teach all three of the grade-six classes, and they're all going to have to do this assignment, aren't they?" I asked.

"Yes, all three," Mrs. Carson confirmed.

"So wouldn't it be simpler if all the classes did the same thing? Wouldn't that be easier for you to explain to them? If that's okay with you, of course."

"I don't see why not," Mrs. Carson agreed.

"I could talk to them about it," I said.

"If you want to talk to them, that would be fine," she said.

"Can I go and talk to them *now*?" I asked.

She looked hesitant.

"That way there would be fewer questions for you to answer," I added.

I saw the hesitation start to lift.

"It won't take me long, and I'll be back in time to finish my email."

She shrugged. "It sounds like a wonderful idea!"

"Thanks. And could I bring somebody with me?"

"Of course."

Kia started to get up.

"Take Lailah with you," Mrs. Carson said.

Kia looked shocked and quickly settled back into her seat, hoping nobody had noticed. Some people had seen her start to get up.

"It might be better if there were three of us. Could—"

"Two is just fine," Mrs. Carson said.

Lailah stood up, pushed in her chair and smiled. There was something about her smile... but she looked sort of...sort of...I don't know, pretty. I glanced over at Kia. She looked as unhappy as Lailah looked happy.

Chapter Six

Hello Ms. Allison,

I wanted to email to thank you for sending us a letter back. Sometimes I think that people just ignore kids, but you didn't. We all appreciated that. You are right that we are really big Raptor fans. You can probably tell by all the emails you are getting from our school. Every student in grade six is sending you a personal email.

That was sort of a lie. It was everybody except Ashley and two of her friends. But seventy-one was almost all the grade sixes, and it wasn't like Ms. Allison would know.

We understand that the Raptors can't visit every school, and that's why we're only asking you to visit ONE school—Clark Boulevard. We think because we are the biggest fans that this would be the best school for Wayne Dawkins to come to. Our school basketball team is called the Clark Cougars. I wish we could be called the Raptors, but I don't get to choose the names. I think that was decided by some principal who was here a long time ago when the school first opened. It's not a bad name, I guess, and both Clark *and* Cougars *start with the same letter. Anyway, I am the co-captain of the team. Last year we were the city champions. This year, so far, we are undefeated.*

Okay, that wasn't even a lie. It was the truth until the next game started. Better if I wrote about something else.

We are still offering a pizza lunch for any Raptors that come, and since you work for the Raptors, you could have pizza too. If you do not like pizza, I could get my mother to make you something special. You could choose, but I would recommend her pasta salad. She makes the best one in the world. It would be really nice to have the Raptors come. We know the Raptors don't give up when they're losing a game, and we don't give up so easily either.

  Your friend,
  Nick

I took a deep breath and then clicked the Send button.

Chapter Seven

Part of me thought that sending the emails was a good idea. Most of me thought it wasn't. The odds were that it wasn't going to make any difference. The only thing that was likely to happen was that people would get their hopes up again and then we'd be told no again. I knew that I wasn't supposed to give up, but with some things, sometimes, it just made sense not to try. Really, if letters didn't work, would emails work? Probably not...unless, maybe, the email went to the right person. And I *had* the email of the right person—a person who *could* help us.

When I arrived home, I went straight to my computer and opened up my Hotmail account. I was going to email Jerome Williams, the former

Raptor fan favorite. Not many people had the email address of a former NBA player. I began typing away. Why hadn't I thought of this earlier?

Hey JYD,
How are you doing? I bet it's a lot hotter where you are than where I am.

Since he retired from the New York Knicks, Jerome and his family had moved to Las Vegas. It was a lot colder here than it was there, for sure.

Everybody in my class wrote letters a couple of weeks ago asking if a Raptor could come to our school, and they said no. Today everybody in grade 6 emailed them to ask the same thing. I know you'd come to visit if you lived here instead of so far away.

I wasn't just saying that. I knew he would come if he could. Jerome was like that. He used to visit schools all the time when he was playing—he and his brother Johnnie—and since he retired, he did it even more. He liked visiting schools and talking to kids. My mother said that he was like a big kid himself—a really *big* kid. She said the same thing about my father, except he wasn't nearly that big. My dad wasn't small—he was six foot three—but compared to Jerome he was pretty short.

I was wondering if you could do me a favor—again. My grades are really good and Kia is doing well also and it's for our whole school, not just for me.

Jerome had done me lots of favors before. He'd come and played ball with us when Kia and I were being bullied by some older guys on a playground court. He'd invited Kia and me to come down to be part of his summer basketball camp—his Boot Camp—in Washington, DC. He'd signed lots of stuff and, even when he was busy, he always answered my emails. Maybe I'd asked him for enough already... maybe I really shouldn't ask him for anything else. Maybe, after this little favor, I wouldn't ask for any more.

I was suddenly feeling guilty. How long had it been since I'd emailed JYD? It had been at least a month. I really didn't like to bother him with lots of emails because I knew how busy he was, but still, now when I was writing I was asking him for something. That wasn't right. But that's what we kids did—we asked for stuff, lots of stuff.

I figured I better butter him up with some basketball talk.

Our team won its first game of the year. We're not too good but we are going to try our best and who knows? If you are up this way, it would be great if you dropped by the school. And if you want to bring somebody along—like Johnnie or anybody else—that would be great.

Okay, maybe I was sort of suggesting that he could bring a Raptor along, but even if it was just him and Johnnie, that would be pretty amazing.

I suggest you guys come on Tuesdays. It's our pizza day and we always have pizza left over... although I've seen you eat pizza and I don't know if we'll have enough left over to feed you.

Your friend,
Nick

   P.S. Do you know Wayne Dawkins? If you do,
could you get him to come for a visit?

Chapter Eight

"And the leading scorer, with twenty-two points, was Kia," the principal said over the P.A.

There were cheers from the class. I noticed that Lailah didn't cheer. She still didn't seem to like Kia any more than Kia liked her.

"...leading our still undefeated Cougars to their third win of the year."

There was an even bigger cheer, and Lailah joined in this time.

"And that concludes our morning announcements. Have a wonderful day at Clark!"

"Let's begin with a period of silent reading," Mrs. Orr said. "Everybody take out a book."

I dug into my desk and grabbed my book. It was about Sherlock Holmes when he was young, and it was called *Eye of the Crow*.

It was so good that I was tempted to bring it out to read at recess...well, tempted, if there wasn't basketball to be played. It *was* a good book... but basketball was a little bit better.

The previous day's game had been a good win. Kia got a whole lot of points from the line. She was repeatedly fouled, partly because she was good, partly because she was a girl, and partly because the other team had a bunch of goof-balls who couldn't handle being schooled by a girl. Three of their starters were gone before the half ended. If they'd been smart and not fouled—or if their coach had been smart and pulled them off when they got their third foul—they probably would have won the game. This was another game we probably should have lost that we somehow managed to win.

What we did lose was another jersey. One of their guys grabbed Bilaal's jersey and practically ripped it off his back. It wasn't that he'd pulled that hard, but the jerseys were so old and worn that they were paper thin. The guy was left with a fistful of jersey and a shocked look on his face. Nobody on our team was shocked. We all knew how old and worn they were. Mr. Roberts said he'd be happy to get us new ones, but the playground repairs were taking all the extra cash that would have been used for things like that. Well, the repairs and all the new computers. Anyway, if we kept losing jerseys like we'd been doing, we might be playing skins and shirts by the end of the year. That wouldn't work so well for Kia.

Lailah had come to the game and cheered me—I mean *us*—on. She was very—

There was a knock on the door, breaking the silence in the room. Before anybody could react, the door opened and Mr. Wills, our caretaker, came in. He was holding a really big brown envelope.

"Special delivery," he said with a big smile.

I liked Mr. Wills. He was a nice guy. I always got the feeling that it was a toss-up between him and the head secretary for who really ran the school. I knew it wasn't the principal or vice-principal.

"This was just brought by a courier and it looks important," Mr. Wills said.

"Just put it on the back table and I'll open it later," Mrs. Orr said.

"*You* shouldn't open it at all," he said, "because it isn't for you."

She looked surprised.

"It says it's for the students of grade six, care of Nick." He pointed at me.

"Me?"

"You're the only Nick we have in grade six, so I figure it must be you. Here you go."

He handed it to me.

"Can I open it now?" I asked Mrs. Orr.

"Well, I'm sure that until you do, nobody is going to be able to concentrate on their reading."

It was a big envelope and it was very stiff, not bendy. I opened it and reached in and pulled out a piece of paper. It was a poster of some sort—a Raptors poster! And there was a second and a third!

"It's from the Raptors," I said, announcing the obvious as I held it up so everybody could see what they had sent.

It was a big poster of all the Raptors players doing different things. In the center was Wayne Dawkins throwing down a dunk and...wait... there was writing on the poster.

"Oh my goodness...they actually signed it," I gasped.

On each picture was a personal signature, all authentic signatures by the Raptors!

"This is amazing! Truly amazing! But who sent them?" Mrs. Orr asked.

"Umm, probably the Raptors," Kia said.

"I sort of guessed that, but who from the Raptors responded?" Mrs. Orr questioned.

I looked deeper into the envelope. Toward the bottom, there was a piece of paper. I pulled it out and started to read. *Hello Nick and the grade-six students. Thank you all for—*

"Read it out loud!" Kia said.

"Oh yeah, sorry. 'Hello Nick and the grade-six students. Thank you all for sending the emails...all seventy-one of them. Your name kept coming up in many of the emails, Nick, so I decided to address this package to you. I hope you like the posters, one for each class, signed by all the players. I told Wayne about what your school did and he was very impressed.'"

Wow. We'd impressed Wayne Dawkins. This was unbelievable. I looked at one of the posters. There was Wayne's signature. He'd actually *touched* this poster.

"Keep reading," Kia said.

"Oh, yeah." I ran my finger down the page to find the spot where I'd stopped. "'I will be sending an email to everybody who emailed us.

You really are a school of true Raptors fans, and I am so disappointed that we can't fit you into this year's Raptors visit schedule, but hopefully, by putting up these posters in your classes, it will feel like you all are part of the Raptor family. Take care, Christina Allison.'"

"Congratulations, Nick and the rest of the class," Mrs. Orr said. "You could have given up after that first letter but you didn't, and now you have something to show for all your efforts."

"So what do we do next, Nicky?" Lailah asked.

"Next?" I asked.

"Yeah, aren't we going to do something else to convince them to come?"

I didn't have any ideas. I looked over at Kia.

"Gee, *Nicky*, tell them your idea," she said, saying "Nicky" in the same tone that Lailah had used. She never called me Nicky. Which one of us was she making fun of? Probably both of us...and what did she mean about me having an idea? I didn't have any ideas.

"Go ahead, *Nicky*, tell us all your idea," Kia said and then smirked at me.

She seemed to be enjoying giving me a hard time—but why? I'd just have to get rid of that smirk. Two could play this game.

"I'd like to tell you, but really it's Kia who had the idea, so maybe she should share the surprise with everybody," I suggested.

Kia's expression went from amused to surprised to angry to blank, all in the space of three seconds. I got her back!

"Go ahead, Kia, tell them."

Kids called out for Kia to tell them her idea.

"I think if I told everybody right now, it wouldn't be a surprise. Besides, it really was *Nicky's* idea as much as mine, so when the time is right, he'll tell everybody."

"I was thinking about some ideas too," Lailah said.

"So was I," Greg added.

"Maybe we could all get together and combine ideas," I suggested. If they both had one, then between the four of us we'd have two ideas instead of none.

"Brainstorming is always a good way to do things," Mrs. Orr said. "But not right now. Right now it's time to go back to silent reading."

Chapter Nine

"Is that everything?" Kia asked.

"I checked the list twice. Everything is in there."

The whole team had got together and come up with ideas. Kia and Lailah had sort of been the cocaptains of the committee. Strange how different the two of them were but how much they had in common. Not that I'd mention that to anybody—especially not them—but take away the extra-long nails and hair products from one and the basketball shoes and jersey from the other, and they had a whole lot in common. Both were very confident and very opinionated. And I wouldn't want to get either of them mad at me. That's why I wouldn't mention the similarities.

After we'd come up with the ideas, we got Mr. Roberts on board as our teacher representative.

Having him take part was like having another kid, but one with adult powers. He was more excited about the ideas than we were, and he seemed to be good at getting the other teachers involved.

It had taken almost two weeks to get our ideas together. And now they were all inside the big idea box. I ran my hand down the side of it. Inside this box might be our best chance of getting a school visit.

"Well, if all the ideas are in there, then let's seal it up," Lailah said.

"Okay, let's just—" Kia stopped and pointed at me.

I looked down. I was still holding the letter that was supposed to go in the box to explain everything.

"Sorry." I went to hand it to her and then pulled back the letter. "Let me just read it through one more time."

I unfolded the letter.

Dear Ms. Allison,

I wanted to write to thank you for the awesome posters. They are up on the walls of all three grade-six classrooms. It was really cool that they were autographed.

Because you sent us some Raptors stuff, we wanted to send you some Raptors stuff we made. Please find enclosed things created by our school for the Raptors.

To show our Raptor spirit, we are sending you original drawings of the Raptors that were done by all of our kindergarten students. There are Raptors paintings that were painted by all of our grade ones. The grade-two students all made posters. The grade-three students all drew portraits of the Raptors players—some are really, really good. The grade-four and grade-five students wrote poems about basketball and the Raptors. Finally, every student in grade six wrote a story called "The Day a Raptor Visited Our School." I guess those are fictional stories, but they would become nonfiction if you send some Raptors to our school.

Maybe you can tell by this letter that we are still hoping that we could become the one school.

There is also a CD of a song called "Raptor Mania." It was written by our music teacher, Mrs. Carson, and sung by the school choir. It is very good. You can use it at halftime or during time-outs if you want. Mrs. Carson has given permission.

There is also one other thing I couldn't put in the box but wanted to tell you about. Last year in grade five we studied government and how democracy works. Recently we decided to test what we learned by having an election. We weren't trying to elect anybody. Instead we held a vote to decide if the majority of our students were in favor of changing the name of our school teams. And they were! Starting next school year, we will have a new name. We will be known as the Clark Raptors—and we will finally have new jerseys in cool Raptors colors.

We would still like to have the Raptors come to our school. And we still have lots of pizza they could eat. And my mother is still willing to make you something else if you don't like pizza.

Your friend,
Nick

"It's good," I said and handed it to Kia.

"So that's everything."

"Yep, everything."

It was everything we'd talked about but not everything I'd hoped for. I was hoping that we'd have something from Jerome—maybe a letter or a promise that he'd call the Raptors himself—

but there was nothing. Not even an answer to my email. Nothing.

That was strange. He *always* answered my emails. Was he upset with me that we hadn't asked *him* to come to the school, or maybe because he thought that I was asking for another favor or...? No, that wasn't like Jerome. He must be busy, or maybe he didn't get the email, or maybe he was on vacation.

I was just glad I hadn't told anybody that I'd emailed Jerome. I'd kept it a secret even from Kia. That way, if something happened it would be a surprise, and if nothing happened, then nobody would be disappointed...or think that I'd failed again.

"Do you think this is going to work?" Lailah asked.

"You miss every shot you don't take," Kia said. "So what have we got to lose?"

Kia was right. There was nothing to lose... except wasting our time, getting people's hopes up for no reason and having everybody blame me when it didn't work. Other than that, there was nothing to lose.

Chapter Ten

I just lay there, in the dark, thinking about our game. We'd won our fifth in a row. I couldn't believe it. I wouldn't have bet on us winning two games the whole season, but here we were five games in and we still hadn't lost. I had to shake my head. Once again we were down by a couple of points with less than a minute to go and we'd pulled it out. Well, Kia had pulled it out. Two baskets and two free throws had turned a potential loss into a win.

I always had trouble sleeping after a game—even if it had been hours and hours before—and tonight was no different. I turned over and my computer made a sound to signal that I had received an email. My mom had told me to turn the computer off so I could get to sleep, but I liked to leave it on. I really didn't like to be in complete darkness. I was too old to have a night-light, but not too old to have a computer that worked like a night-light.

I rolled out of bed and went over to investigate. Maybe I should just check the message. It could be from Kia. No, it was almost midnight and she'd be in bed and asleep.

That made me even more curious. Who would be emailing me at this time of night? I clicked on the screen.

Hey Nick,

It's me, JYD! Sorry it took so long for me to get back to you, but I'm on the other side of the world right now. Far, far away from home. I'm writing to you from South Africa! Johnnie and I are here with the NBA Basketball Without Borders program. I am now an NBA Cares ambassador who travels to different countries to promote this game we both love.

I am sure that you have seen the commercials during NBA games that say NBA Cares. Well, small groups of former and current players visit different countries to support young people, meet political figures and open learn-and-play centers. We dedicate basketball courts in some communities as well as host a basketball camp for the best young players from all across that country.

Johnnie spoke today to some American and Canadian students attending the private school that is hosting our Basketball Without Borders camp about serving others, just like their parents who represent their countries as diplomats.

We also talk a lot to the kids who live here all the time. Over here the young people have so many challenges that get in the way of them reaching their dreams. But what has shocked me is that even though so many kids here have been affected by AIDS and lost their parents, they still smile every day and ask for very little. There's one kid, his name is Tulani, and he's been like a guide to us. He plays basketball in bare feet because he and the other kids can't afford shoes. He really loves the game but has no shoes to wear to school or to play ball in. There are so many young kids here with no shoes. If my feet weren't three times as big as his, I'd give him my shoes. I wish there was some way to help him and the others.

Hey, you were asking me for some help with getting the Raptors to your school, right? Have they responded yet?

Well, I gotta go now. Our bus is about to leave and I have to pay for my computer time before they leave me behind.

Just remember, when asking the Raptors to do something for you, try to show that you and your classmates care about others, just like the NBA cares about its fans. That will separate your request from all the others. Good luck.

I'll email you later if I can,

JYD

Well, that explained why I hadn't heard from him. It was so amazing that he was in Africa. Of course, that also meant that he wasn't really able to help us out at this time.

"Nick, you should be asleep. And I hope that computer is off," shouted my mom from the other room.

I quickly pushed the button to turn the computer off. "It's off...good night," I replied.

Chapter Eleven

The gym was alive with the sound of squeaking shoes and bouncing balls. I loved those sounds. We had started playing basketball in gym class, so it was like getting double the practice. I really did love basketball.

Lailah was at the far end of the gym. She was coming to all our games now. It was good to have fans, but having her there made me a little nervous.

Lailah put up a shot. It dropped—nothing but net. Nice shot. Or lucky shot.

"Pretty unbelievable, huh?" Kia asked.

I was jolted out of my thoughts. I felt so embarrassed that Kia had caught me looking.

"What?" I asked.

"Her."

Lailah put up a second shot and it dropped. "Lucky," I said.

"What are you talking about?" Kia asked.

"What are *you* talking about?"

"Isn't it obvious? The fancy clothing, the strange, thinks-she's-*so*-cool hairstyle, those super-long, ridiculous nails, and now she's *trying* to play basketball."

Lailah put up a third shot and it dropped as well.

"Lucky shot," Kia said.

"That's what I meant, but that's three in a row so maybe it's more than luck."

"Even you've made three in a row."

"Funny." But semi-true. I could take Kia one-on-one, but in a straight shooting match, especially free throws, she was hard to beat.

Lailah dropped in her fourth shot. If that was luck, she was very lucky. But honestly, her shooting form was really good...almost perfect.

"You better not get into a game of horse against her. If you lose, it might be even *more* embarrassing for you to be around her," Kia said.

"I can take her...what do you mean *more* embarrassing?"

"Nothing. She just made her fifth shot in a row," Kia replied.

"Maybe it should be you who's afraid to play against her...or...Come with me."

I led Kia over to where Lailah was shooting. She put up another shot and made her sixth in a row.

"Nice shot," I said.

"I'm more than a pretty face, you know."

She was definitely a pretty face. I felt myself starting to blush. "You can shoot the ball. Do you play basketball?"

"I used to."

"You used to?" I asked.

"I like watching it on TV, and playing it is okay, I guess. And I do like coming to *your* games."

She smiled sweetly and I started blushing harder. I couldn't let anybody notice that—I snapped myself back to reality.

As she was talking, she was dribbling the ball and looking at *me* and not the ball. Then she crossed it over through her legs! She had crazy ball control. That put her ahead of almost everybody on the school team. I thought about going away and talking to Kia first about what I was going to say next, but I knew she'd object and get mad. So I just went for it. "You know, we still have a spot open on the basketball team."

Kia's eyes widened in shock. She obviously hadn't seen that one coming, but she quickly recovered. "That's Greg's spot. He'll be back in a game or two."

"Even with him we still have one spot open. We can carry twelve."

"Do you really think I'm good enough?" Lailah asked.

"You shoot better than most of the guys on the team."

She hesitated. "I know, but...it just seems so strange—a girl playing on the boys' team."

Kia made a huffing sound.

"I was thinking about trying out for the girls' team, maybe."

"You can play for both," I said. "The girls' season starts when our season ends."

"Does she do that?" Lailah asked, pointing at Kia.

"She does not," Kia answered.

"But she could," I said. "You could too. I don't see any reason why you couldn't try out for—"

"Except for those nails," Kia said, cutting me off. "There's no way you'd be allowed to play with those nails because you could scratch somebody."

"They're fake," she said. "I could easily take them off and get them replaced after the season."

"So you're going to try out?" I asked.

"Maybe."

"You could talk to Mr. Roberts, or I could talk to him for you, if you want."

"That would be so sweet of you." She paused. "And Nicky, thanks for thinking about me."

I felt my whole body blush.

Chapter Twelve

Mr. Wills appeared at the classroom door, holding a large box. He knocked and walked in. Mrs. Orr stopped teaching and we all turned toward him.

"Second delivery for Nick," he said.

For a split second I had the terrible thought that it was the box we'd sent to the Raptors and they'd just sent it back to us. But I could see it was a different box. It was a little bit smaller and a slightly different color cardboard.

"It's from the Raptors," he said as he put it down on my desk.

"What is it?" I gasped.

"Only one way to find out. Open it."

I stood up and started to try to undo the tape sealing it shut, but it was pretty strong.

"Let me," Mr. Wills said. He pulled out a box cutter and ran it along the top of the box, splitting the tape in two.

I opened the flaps. It was filled with those little white packing noodles. I pushed some aside and there was a basketball peeking up at me. I pulled it out. It was a beautiful, leather, official NBA ball with the Spalding emblem on it!

I held it up high for the whole class to see. "And look, it's signed!"

The class reacted with cheers.

I rotated it slowly to look at all the signatures. I quickly found Wayne's, and beside his signature he'd written #4, his jersey number.

"Is there a letter?" Mrs. Orr asked.

I looked into the box and rustled around in the noodles. "I don't see one."

Mr. Wills tapped the side of the box. "It's right here."

I spun the box around. There was an envelope attached to the side. I pulled it off, opened it up and unfolded the page.

"Read it out loud," Kia suggested.

I took a deep breath. Here we go again with all this reading. I really liked reading but not necessarily out loud and in front of a whole audience.

"'Hello, Nick and everybody else at Clark Boulevard Public School. Thank you for all the wonderful paintings, poems, posters, drawings and stories, not to mention the great song. In all my years in this job I have never seen a school so committed to the Raptors, and it's great that your school teams will be called the Raptors next year. We would like you to use this signed basketball as your official school ball and place it in your school's trophy case.'"

That's right, the ball wasn't just for me, even though the box was addressed to me—and everybody else really. It was a school ball.

"'Since you have shown that you are really a one-in-a-million school—well, let's make that a one-in-a-thousand—I would like to offer a visit by a Raptor—'"

Everybody jumped to their feet and burst into screams and cheers before I could read the rest of the sentence. Right now they were all excited and happy, but I knew different. I'd read a few words ahead.

Kia looked at me questioningly. She knew something was wrong.

"'...by a Raptor sometime in the future!'" I yelled out. "Sometime in the future!" I yelled louder, and the cheering suddenly stopped and the room got quieter again—deadly quiet.

"'I would like to offer a visit by a Raptor *sometime in the future*. We might even be able to send the mascot this year. I just wish there was a spot available for a Raptors player, but we can't schedule any more visits this year and we don't pre-schedule visits for next year. We encourage your school to contact us again in June, when we start to schedule visits for next year. While there are no guarantees, Clark Boulevard will certainly be considered. If we're able to fit you into the schedule, I'd like you to save me a big piece of pizza! Go Raptors Go! Christina.'"

"That is wonderful news!" Mrs. Orr beamed. "It sounds like somebody from the Raptors will be coming next year or even this year!"

"This year would only be the mascot, not a Raptor," Kia said.

"That's still exciting," Mrs. Orr said. "And he is a very good mascot, isn't he?"

"Yeah, I really like him," I admitted. "He does lots of cool things...but it's not like having a Raptor."

"They did say there was the possibility of a player coming to the school."

"*Next* year, when none of us are going to be at this school," Kia added.

Mrs. Orr looked surprised. "I'm sorry, I didn't even think about that. You'll all be in middle school...but it is wonderful news for the rest of the school."

"But not for us," Kia added. "We'll all be gone."

"Perhaps we can arrange for you all to come back that day to visit," Mrs. Orr suggested.

"Seventy-five of us?" Kia asked.

"I'm sure we can work it out."

"That is if they even come," Greg said. "She was saying maybe, no guarantees."

He was right.

"Regardless, you all should still be proud of yourselves. You not only wrote to a business but kept on writing and doing things until you achieved your goal," Mrs. Orr said.

She was right—we had sort of achieved our goal. The Raptors mascot was coming. Maybe.

The whole room was quiet. We'd tried everything, but we'd still lost. Or had we tried everything? Maybe we could...could...I had nothing left. We'd already done everything, and I was out of ideas. I looked over at Kia. She held up her hands and shrugged.

Chapter Thirteen

"Okay, everybody, let's settle down!" Mr. Roberts yelled, and the change room became quiet.

"Congratulations on our sixth win of the season," he said to accompanying hoots and hollers.

"That was a real team effort. We kept clawing our way back like cougars."

"Or like Raptors!" Kia said.

"Or like Raptors," Mr. Roberts said. "Either way, there was no quit in anybody, and we won the way we've won all year. Never quitting, never giving up and coming from behind to win at the end."

It had been another nail-biter. A three-point win at the end after being down by ten points when there was less than ten minutes left.

Somehow it was relaxing playing on a team where we weren't supposed to win but kept winning. This win made us six and two for the season. Not a perfect year but way beyond where we should have been.

"This was a real team effort," Mr. Roberts said again, "with efforts from every member of the team, including our newest member, Lailah."

She got up and bowed, and people clapped and cheered. Lailah had scored four points, and since we won by three, it was really her points that won it for us.

"It was also great to have Greg playing his second game of the season!" Mr. Roberts said.

More cheers erupted and Greg waved. He was still a little rusty after being gone so long, but he'd played more minutes and better than he had the first game. He'd chipped in a couple of points and some rebounds, and, more importantly, having him back let Kia and me take a little more rest during the game. That meant at the end we still had something in the tank, and that was a big part of why we'd come back.

"And that was another outstanding performance from our co-captains. Nick, with sixteen points, and our leading scorer, Kia, with eighteen."

Again there was more cheering.

"Between the play of Kia and Lailah, it looks like what this team really needs is more girls," Mr. Roberts said. "It must be nice for you, Kia, to finally have another girl on the team."

"Yeah, sure," she said. She didn't sound that enthusiastic.

The two of them had learned to sort of get along together. At least they weren't openly fighting anymore. It was all more subtle now—a look or expression, or things that they *didn't* say. Like the way Kia didn't say how wonderful it was to have Lailah play.

"I'm so proud of this team," Mr. Roberts said.

"Proud enough to give us the morning off?" Greg asked.

"The reason this team keeps winning is that we don't take any time off. Not a minute off, and not a practice off. I'll see you all tomorrow at seven thirty sharp. Great game and go home!"

I picked up my bag and followed everybody out of the change room, down the hall and out into the schoolyard. Parents were waiting to pick up kids at the door, and others were going to walk home.

I looked at my watch. My mother would be here in ten minutes to pick up Kia and me. She'd only been to one of my games all year. Her new job meant that she wasn't as available to come to games. Before this she'd basically been at every game I'd ever played, and it was strange not to have her there. And most of the time, even if she couldn't come, my father would have been there. But he had hardly even been home in the last month—his job had him traveling all over the place.

It was a bit strange not to have them at the games, but it was okay. In some ways it felt like I was a little kid with his mommy and daddy cheering for him all the time. But I wasn't a kid anymore. I *was* in grade six.

Kia and I walked toward the swings. No need to talk about where we were going. When you'd been friends as long as we had, there was often no need to talk at all. We just knew what the other was thinking. We both took a swing, although I was so tired I didn't feel like swinging, just sitting.

"So the Raptors aren't coming," Kia said.

"Doesn't look like it. At least not coming this year when it will do any good for us. Although maybe we'll get the mascot," I added. "He is the best mascot in the league."

"I was thinking that there still is one more thing we haven't tried," she said.

"There is? What?"

"What if we asked JYD to help?"

"I already thought of that," I said.

"You did?"

I nodded my head. "I emailed him."

"And you didn't tell me?"

"I guess I forgot," I lied. "He said to say hello to you."

"And you forgot that too? What did he say?"

"He wished us luck."

"And is he going to help? You know, make a call or something?"

"I'm not sure it's that easy. There might not be phones where he is."

"I'm pretty sure Las Vegas has phones," Kia said.

"He wasn't in Vegas. He was in Africa, and then he was going to China."

"Wow, that's exciting. Is this like a trip with his family?" Kia asked.

"Johnnie's with him, but the rest of the people are part of his NBA family. He's one of a group of retired NBA legends and current WNBA players with the Basketball Without Borders program."

"I've heard of that, but, you know, I think there are phones in Africa and China. I think most of the phones here are made in China."

I shrugged. "Yeah...I guess. I just didn't really, exactly ask him to help us...much."

"What does that mean?" she asked.

"It just felt bad, pestering him all the time for favors."

"It's not pestering him. You should email him again and ask him to help get a Raptor here."

"*You* could email him if you wanted," I suggested. "It's not like I'm the only one with his email address."

"Well..."

"Well what?"

"When you mention it, maybe it is asking him for another favor, like we're taking advantage of him."

"Exactly."

"So unless we can come up with another idea, the Raptors aren't coming to our school," Kia said. "You got any other ideas?" she asked.

"Nothing. We've tried everything."

"I guess," Kia agreed.

Lailah came out the door, waved and started walking toward us.

"Hi, guys," she said. "That was a lot of—"

Her words were lost in the roar of the plane passing overhead.

"I can't get over how loud they are," she said.

"You get used to it," Kia said.

"I don't think I could *ever* get used to it."

"You won't be here long enough to get used to it," I said. "Next year is middle school and we're gone."

"And the Raptors come," Kia added. "That really sucks."

"Don't you have *any* other ideas, Nicky?" Lailah asked.

I shook my head. "I got noth—"

A second plane came overhead and the engines again overwhelmed everything. There were a lot of them today. Sometimes it would be days and days without planes, and then other days it seemed like every two minutes. It all depended on which runway they were using, which depended on the direction of the wind. Today the wind was coming from the right—or I guess wrong—direction, so we had lots of air traffic overhead.

Lailah was waving up at the plane as it passed.

"What are you doing?" Kia snapped.

"Just waving, saying hello, being friendly."

"They can't see you, you know," Kia said. She shook her head and had a look of disgust on her face.

"Maybe they can," Lailah argued.

"They can see the school and the playground for sure," I said. "I even saw my house once when we were flying back from New York."

"Then maybe they *could* see me," Lailah said.

"You're slightly smaller than a house...especially without those ridiculous nails!"

"There was nothing ridiculous about my nails!" Lailah protested. "Nothing."

"I heard that the field is going to be ready by the end of the week," I said, changing the subject completely.

My statement was greeted by silence.

"Did you see that they delivered all the sod today?" I pointed at the big wooden pallets loaded with pieces of sod. It would be great to have grass on the field and be able to play out there.

There was still no response from either of them.

"I wonder how long it will be after they put down the grass before we'll be able to go out on it? Do either of you know?"

Nobody volunteered an answer. Great...I was having a conversation with myself and it wasn't even a good conversation!

Another plane came in. It was even lower and louder. Right now I welcomed the sound to break the silence.

Lailah started jumping up and down and yelling and waving so loudly that even the sound of the plane didn't drown her out completely. The plane passed.

"I'm sure they could see me *that* time," Lailah said.

"Yeah, and I'm sure they could *hear* you as well," Kia added.

"I think they could see me. What do you think, Nicky?"

"Me? You want to know what I think?"

"Yes."

"Yeah, *Nicky*, what do you think?" Kia questioned.

They both stood there staring at me. Lailah was smiling and Kia was scowling. They were both waiting for an answer—an answer that was guaranteed to make at least one of them angry with me. I tried to think of an answer that would please them both, but I realized that was impossible.

Then, out of nowhere, an answer came into my mind. It brought a smile to my face.

Chapter Fourteen

"I need the whole team to come back to school tonight," I said.

"What?" Kia questioned.

"I need everybody to come back to school."

"What are you going to do, have a vote to decide if the planes can see Lailah?" Kia asked.

"No, of course not. But I do need everybody, or as many people as we can get, to come here for six thirty. That should give us enough time before it gets dark."

"Enough time for what?" Kia asked.

"Yeah, for what?" Lailah echoed.

I smiled. "It's a surprise."

"I love surprises," Lailah said.

"I think that his surprise isn't going to involve makeup, fake nails or fancy clothes," Kia snapped.

Lailah started to say something but I jumped in. "Clothes *are* important. Nobody should wear anything that's fancy or expensive."

"I'm sure Kia won't have any trouble with that," Lailah said.

"And Kia," I said, cutting in before she could answer. "Could you get the message out to everybody and ask them to come back here?"

"Why don't you call them?" she asked.

"I'm going to be busy getting things ready."

"What things?" she asked.

"If I told you that, it wouldn't be a surprise. Will you call everybody, please?"

"I could call every—," Lailah started to say.

"I'll call," Kia said, cutting her off.

"There's my mother," Lailah said.

A fancy blue suv had pulled up to the school. A woman got out—she had wavy hair and was very well dressed. She looked and dressed like Lailah, and she waved in our direction.

"I have to go," Lailah said. "I'll be back at six thirty." She smiled at me and then walked away.

"She could have waved back at *her mother*," Kia said. "She could have seen her because she wasn't in a plane."

"I thought it would be better between you two once you were teammates."

"Since when do you have to like everybody who's on your team?" Kia asked.

"Well..."

"Well what?"

"It's not just that you don't like her, but that you *really, really* don't like her."

"I don't like phony people," Kia said.

"She's not phony."

"What would you know?" Kia questioned. "I just can't handle the way she acts. And what's even worse is the way the guys in the class act when she's around."

"What do you mean?"

"You probably didn't notice because *you* act the same way."

"What are you talking about?" I demanded.

"'Oh *Nicky*...look at *meee*...aren't I *sooo* special...and you're *sooo* smart and such a good basketball player...you're like my hero!'"

"She's never said that."

"It must have sounded something like her, because you did know I was trying to sound like her."

She had a point, but I wasn't going to give her that point.

"Maybe she didn't use those words, but it's the attitude, the goofy clothes with goofy nails. If you can't see it, then you're as stupid as everybody else."

"If I'm so stupid, how come I came up with an awesome idea?"

Her expression softened. "What's your idea, and why do you want everybody to come here?" she asked.

"I guess you'll have to wait until six thirty to find out."

"Come on, you can tell me. You know I hate surprises."

"I'd really like to tell you, but I'm a little stupid and the idea just slipped from my mind. I'm sure I'll remember by six thirty though. I'm not *that* stupid."

Chapter Fifteen

I looked at my watch. It was almost six thirty. At first I'd been worried that I wouldn't have things ready before they arrived. Now I was worried that nobody was going to show up. It was a good plan, and I'd done all the preplanning and the work to set it up. I just hoped we had enough people willing to help. I guessed that depended on how many people showed up. If Kia got in touch with everybody and they all came, we could definitely do it.

Then I had a terrible thought. When we dropped Kia off at her house, she was still angry at me. That was partly because I refused to tell her my plan. Really, I didn't want to tell her with my mother in the car. But getting Kia angry was never a smart thing to do. Maybe she wasn't coming back. Maybe she'd decided not to call anybody. Then it would be only Lailah and me, and no matter how hard we worked, we wouldn't be able to complete the project with just two of us.

A car pulled into the parking lot. It was Kia's parents' car. It stopped and Kia got out—and Lailah got out the other side! That was the last thing I expected, the two of them sharing a ride. As they started to walk over, two other cars pulled in and more members of the team climbed out.

Kia had obviously made the phone calls. I felt bad for thinking that she wouldn't have done it. Even when she was mad at me, she would still follow through on something she'd committed to doing.

As everybody walked over, I noticed that while Lailah and Kia were in grungy clothes, all of the guys were wearing our school basketball jerseys and their basketball shoes. Greg was even carrying a ball. What did they think was going on?

More cars pulled up and more of the guys got out—all of them wearing their jerseys.

"Hey, Nick," Greg said, "where's Mr. Roberts?"

"At home I guess."

"What's he doing at home?"

"He usually doesn't talk to me much about his personal life," I replied.

Greg looked as confused by my answer as I was confused by his questions.

"But how can we have a practice without Mr. Roberts?"

I looked at Kia.

"I told them all that we were having a practice to get them here," she explained.

"Why did you tell them that?"

"I couldn't tell them what was really going to happen because I didn't know," she said. "Somebody wasn't willing to share it...remember?"

"You mean there isn't going to be a practice?" Greg asked.

"No practice."

"So what are we doing here?" Greg questioned.

"It's something really cool, right, Nick?" Lailah asked.

"Hopefully. Let's wait until everybody is here, and then I'll explain it to everybody at the same time."

"Where do you want this one?" Kia asked. She and Lailah were carrying a piece of sod between them.

"Here, I'll take it."

I took the sod and dropped it to the ground, right inside the line. I unrolled it, pushed it into place and then tapped it with my foot so it was exactly in the right position.

"How many more pieces do you think we need?" Kia asked.

"Maybe twenty or so...no more than thirty pieces."

"That's good. I'm getting tired," Kia said.

"And dirty. Really dirty," Lailah added. "I'm never going to get the dirt out from under my nails."

"Lucky thing your nails are a lot shorter now," Kia said, and they both started laughing, together, like friends.

"I'll go and get another piece," Lailah said.

She left, leaving Kia and me alone.

"You two seem awfully friendly."

"We are teammates."

"Weren't you the one, just a few hours ago, who told me you don't have to be friends just because you're teammates?" I asked.

"Yeah, but things can change. She called and asked for a ride and we started talking."

"And what did you talk about?" I asked.

"For starters, did you know that she sort of thought that you and I were like boyfriend and girlfriend?"

"That is so stupid! You're a girl and you're my friend—my *best* friend—but you're not my girlfriend. More like my sister."

"That's what I told her. Anyway, we are in the same class, and we are teammates and the only two girls on the team. And it's not her fault that boys act goofy around her...well, not completely her fault."

"I still don't know what you're talking about. I don't act any different around—"

Devon came up with a piece of sod. "Where do you want this one, boss?"

"Any place inside the line works."

Greg was right behind him with another piece.

"We're not going to get in trouble for this, are we?" Greg asked.

"I don't think so."

"How would this get us in trouble?" Kia questioned.

"It is sort of like we're doing vandalism," Greg said.

"Vandalism?" Kia said, sounding offended. "We're not breaking anything, or stealing anything. It's not like we're spray painting a wall."

"She's right. We're not even close to a wall." Greg still looked worried.

"If there is a problem—and there won't be—but if there is, then I'll say it was all my idea and my fault," I said. "I'll take all the blame."

"Thanks, that's nice of you." He dropped the piece of sod he was holding and started to put it into place.

Kia moved close to me. "Do you think we *will* get in trouble?" she whispered to me.

"Probably not, but if we do, I'll just ask for forgiveness," I said, giving her Mr. Roberts's line. "The more important thing is whether this is going to work."

"It looks good...I guess."

"I just wish we had a better angle," I said.

"We could climb on the roof."

"Not high enough and too far away. And we still couldn't tell if it's big enough."

"I guess you're right," she said. "We'll just have to wait and see."

"First we have to finish up. Let's get going. There's not much left to do, but there's not much light left either."

Chapter Sixteen

I had one eye on my work and one eye on the window. The little slice of sky that I could see was too small and the angle was all wrong for me to see much. Why couldn't my desk be on the other side of the class by the windows?

I deliberately pressed down hard on my pencil and the tip snapped off. I got up and walked toward the pencil sharpener, which was on the window ledge. I walked as quietly and slowly as possible. It wasn't that I didn't want to disturb anybody doing their math, but I didn't want Mrs. Orr to notice me. She was working at her desk, eyes down. If I moved silently, then maybe she wouldn't—

"Nick?" Mrs. Orr said.

"Sharpener," I replied. I held the pencil up like I was showing proof of where I was going and what I was going to do when I got there.

"Isn't this your third or fourth trip to the sharpener this morning?"

"I haven't really been counting," I lied. It was my fourth. "But I'm sure you're right. It has been a lot. This must be the worst pencil in the *world*."

"I have extra pencils."

It was Lailah. She smiled and I felt all gooey inside. I appreciated her offer, but I didn't need a pencil—I needed to *sharpen* a pencil. Then I noticed the pencil she was holding out for me was brand-new and *really* needed to be sharpened.

I walked over to get the pencil.

"Thanks," I said, trying to sound casual.

"Any planes?" she whispered.

I wasn't even aware she knew why I was going over there so often, but obviously she was.

I shook my head. "Not that I've seen."

I went over to the window and started to sharpen the pencil—very slowly. I figured I had to make this trip my last because I certainly wasn't going to be able to come back here again.

I bent down slightly so I had a better angle out the window and could see more of the sky and—there was one! A plane was coming in just to the side of the school, just to the side of the field. Perfect, just perfect. Well…assuming it was big enough.

I finished sharpening the pencil and returned to my seat.

For the first part of the morning I'd been worried that the whole plan, all of our effort, was for nothing and it might not work. Now, having seen the plane, I was worried that it *was* going to work.

The twelve of us stood on the basketball court in the schoolyard, but there was no basketball going on. Instead we stood there watching as planes flew overhead.

"Here comes another one!" Kia exclaimed.

It was a big American Airlines plane.

"It's almost right over top of us," Lailah said.

"It might be better if it was a little off to the side," I added. "But either way it's good."

The plane passed by, its engines roaring, and we all laughed and yelled and waved. Even Kia waved. I was going to say something about her doing that, but I thought it was better to just ignore the whole thing. The two of them seemed to be getting along.

Plane after plane kept coming in for a landing. The wind was blowing from the perfect direction to cause the planes to use the runway that brought them right over top of us. Most of the people living in the homes around here would much rather it was blowing from a different direction. But today, that wind direction and those planes flying over were perfect.

I'd had some terrible moments last night—after we'd done all the work and I was home lying in bed—thinking that sometimes there were days and days when no planes came over the school. Today could have been one of those days. Tomorrow could be one of those days, and by the time the wind was blowing in the right direction, the whole thing could have been taken apart. I would have put everybody to work for nothing. I shuddered at that thought. But none of that mattered now as another plane came into view.

This time there was a bigger cheer. I looked around. There were lots of kids reacting to the plane overhead. Were they just imitating us or...?

"Did anybody mention what we did to anybody else?" I asked.

No one answered, the silence submerged by the roar of the plane overhead. Nobody seemed to want to look at me either.

"I told a couple of people," Greg admitted.

"Me too," Devon added.

Everybody else nodded in agreement.

"It was supposed to be a secret," I said.

"It doesn't matter, because it won't be a secret for long," Kia said. "Besides, what can it hurt?"

I didn't have an answer for that, although I guess part of me still worried about what Greg had mentioned the day before. This *was* sort of vandalism, and we could get in trouble.

I stopped watching the planes and started watching the schoolyard. It was like a ripple as more and more people began to react to the planes coming in. It was like the "secret" was being passed on from person to person until everybody was in on it. I remembered my mother once told me that as soon as a second person knew your secret, it wasn't a secret anymore. We'd started with twelve and now it looked like it was six hundred.

The bell rang and we all started filing into our lines to go in. As we stood there, waiting to enter, another plane came over and the lines erupted in cheering.

"You kids certainly seem to like airplanes," Mrs. Carson said. She was on yard duty.

"Airplanes *are* pretty exciting," Kia agreed.

Chapter Seventeen

The phone rang and I picked it up on the first ring.

"Turn on TSN," Kia said.

"I'm watching *Sports Desk*."

We had an ongoing argument about which was the better station for sports.

"Good for you, but my guess is that you're *not* the next story up on *Sports Desk*," she said.

"What?"

"They just went to commercial but they said that they're coming back with a story about us."

"Us? They mentioned us?"

"Not us, like Nick and Kia, but us as in what we did."

"Are you sure it's about us?"

"Just turn it on."

"Of course I will."

"And Nick, which station is the best again?" Kia asked.

She started laughing and I hung up the phone. I grabbed the converter and punched in the numbers. It was still on commercial for a fancy car, which quickly drove off, and then the commercial ended and we were back to the show. The two hosts—both former professional athletes—were wearing suits and ties and sitting behind a big desk.

"Welcome back. I'm Frankie Horton and with me is my good buddy, Will Strickland."

"It's great to be here." He turned directly into the camera. "You're going to *love* this next story," Frankie said.

"It certainly brought a smile to my face," Will agreed. "Today support for our hometown Raptors reached new heights."

The screen changed to show the view of our schoolyard as seen from an airplane. My mouth dropped open—it was perfect!

"Passengers flying into Toronto today were greeted by a gigantic sign cheering on our Raptors," Will said. "Those letters that you're seeing on the screen, are over twenty feet high, and the whole thing is one hundred and twenty feet long."

There it was on the TV screen for everybody watching the show to see—*GO RAPTORS GO* in giant grass letters, brilliant green against the brown of the dirt. It looked like it slanted a little bit to the side, and the *O* in the word *Raptors* was slightly smaller than the rest of the letters, but other than that it was perfect. I'd been so worried that I'd done it wrong, even though I'd used a measuring tape when I'd drawn the outline of the letters in the dirt—but there it was, almost letter-perfect!

"This scene was created in the schoolyard of Clark Boulevard Public School, where the grass on the field is being replaced with new sod.

"At first we thought we had some workers from the sod company to thank—"

"No, no, it's us!" I screamed at the TV.

"But we've subsequently found out the *true* story," one of them said.

I could only hope it *was* the true story.

"In an exclusive TSN story, we take you live to the Air Canada Centre, where our reporter, Julia Elizabeth, is standing by."

There were two women standing, one of them—I guess Julia—holding a microphone.

"Hello, I'm here at the ACC with Christina Allison, Director of Community and Public Relations with the Raptors."

So *that's* what she looked like. She was a lot younger than I'd thought.

"So, Christina, you told us that you might have some insights about the creation of what we're calling the Stonehenge of Raptors signs."

"Yes, Julia. At first we had no more of an idea than anybody else about who created this sign," she said. "But when we found out the location—the schoolyard of Clark Boulevard Public School—then I knew immediately."

"And?" Julia asked.

"We've had a lot of contact with the students of that school."

"What sort of contact?"

"They have sent us letters, emails, posters, paintings, drawings and written songs, and they have even changed the name of the school teams. They are probably the biggest Raptors fans in the city. And now they have created the biggest Raptors sign in history."

"It certainly is the biggest one any of us have ever seen. Maybe the Guinness World Records people should be contacted."

I hadn't even thought of that—that would be so cool.

"So, Christina, who do we have to thank for this wonderful Raptors sign?" Julia asked.

"The whole effort has been led by one of the captains of the basketball team, a young man in grade six named Nick."

Part of me wanted to cheer and part of me wanted to climb under the bed and hide. It was unbelievable that I was being mentioned on TSN, but also terrible that I was being mentioned. Now, for better or worse, everybody knew or was soon going to know. Everybody, including my parents, teachers, the principal and the guys who were in charge of the sod, would know. Boy, could there ever be trouble.

"Of course, I'm sure he didn't do it by himself," Christina went on. "This was probably the effort of the entire basketball team."

That was so good she'd mentioned everybody. We all deserved the credit...and we could all share the blame as well.

"They sound like tremendous fans of the Raptors," Julia said.

"That school is one in a thousand. And because of that I'm going to make a special offer to them."

I jumped out of my seat. It had worked! They were coming to our school!

"I will be contacting their school tomorrow to offer them an invitation for the entire Clark Boulevard basketball team to attend this weekend's game. They will be our very special guests and will watch the game from the owners' private box!"

I screamed out in excitement. This was incredible! Not just a game but seeing it from the owners' box! Unbelievable!

"So, we hope that the captain of the team, Nick, and the rest of the members of the Clark Boulevard team are out there watching," Julia said. "And now, back to Will and Frankie."

I slumped back onto my bed and the phone rang. I reached for it and then hesitated. It could be Kia. It could be somebody else who wasn't so happy about what we did. I looked at the call display before I decided to answer. It was Kia. I picked up the phone.

Chapter Eighteen

When I told Greg that I'd be the one to get in trouble if anyone did, I was just talking to make him feel better. Now, as I sat in the principal's office along with my mother, I wasn't feeling like that was such a wonderful plan. The only other kid here was Kia, and it wasn't hard to notice that neither of *her* parents was here.

I wasn't sure whether I wanted to yell out that it was my idea, so I could get Kia off, or claim it was a whole team effort so that the blame could be spread around a little. But really, this last part had been my idea alone. If there was trouble coming, it should just be coming for me. For better or worse, I'd have to accept whatever happened. Besides, being mentioned on TV made it all worth it...assuming I wasn't going to get in too much trouble.

"Thanks for coming on such short notice," Mr. Waldman said to my mother.

"I'm glad to be here."

"And I appreciate you two giving up a recess."

Like we had a choice—*Yeah, I know the principal wants to see us...Tell him I'm going outside to play instead.*

"Sure, no problem," Kia said.

She looked as nervous as I felt. This wasn't a good sign.

"Well, Nicholas, do you have anything you want to say to start the meeting?" Mr. Waldman asked.

Instantly I thought about that whole "asking for forgiveness" thing and how that might work, but I had to wait for the right time to say it.

I just shook my head. Anything I could say could only make things worse.

"In that case, perhaps I'll start," he said. "This has all been a whirlwind of activity. Certainly things moved more quickly and in different directions than any of us could have foreseen."

This might be the spot to say I was sorry. I opened my mouth and—

"And that's why we all owe Kia, and especially Nick, a big thank-you," Mr. Waldman said.

My jaw dropped open. That was the last thing in the world I had expected to hear. I looked at Kia. She looked equally shocked.

"Um...you're welcome," I mumbled.

"Without your persistence, none of this would have happened."

"We're proud of them," my mother said.

"It was really more Nick than me," Kia said.

That was nice of her—unless there was some trouble still coming.

"You have both always shown great leadership," Mr. Waldman said. "Both on and off the basketball court."

"Thanks, but it wasn't just us. It was the whole team."

It really wasn't just me. And besides, there still might be some trouble to come, and I wouldn't mind setting the tone for spreading that blame around if it came to that.

"So...we're not in any trouble...right?" Kia asked. She looked pleadingly from our principal to my mother.

"You're not in trouble," Mr. Waldman said. "But you *could* have been in big trouble. While there was no damage done, the company responsible for the sod could have involved the police if they chose to do so."

"The police?" I gasped.

"You didn't have permission to move their sod."

"But they're not doing that, are they?" I asked. "They aren't getting the police involved, right?"

"No, they're not. Did you see the owners on TV last night?"

I shook my head.

"Yes, I caught them on the news," my mother said. "The owner seemed so proud, you would have thought they'd done it themselves."

"I guess you can't buy publicity like that," Mr. Waldman said. "In fact they're so happy that they actually agreed to keep the sod letters in place for the next week, and they're even going to water it to keep it all green and alive."

"That's wonderful!" I exclaimed.

"It does delay the completion and use of the field for a few days, but so be it," Mr. Waldman said. "Now we need to turn to the more immediate issues." He turned directly to my mother. "Thank you for offering to drive some of the team down to the game this weekend."

"That's why you're here?" I asked my mother.

"Why did you think I was here?" she responded.

"I really wasn't sure. I thought maybe I was in trouble."

"As I said, you *could* have been in trouble," Mr. Waldman said, "but we really do think it's been a wonderful boost for the students and staff, not to mention all the positive publicity it's brought to the school. My phone has been ringing off the hook all morning."

"Our phone too," my mother added.

Obviously I hadn't been getting phone calls in class, but everybody in the school had been coming up and talking to me. I couldn't believe how excited the basketball team was about it. No, wait—I *could* believe it because I was pretty excited too.

"Newspapers and TV reporters kept calling to try to get information or arrange interviews or say congratulations. Great stuff," Mr. Waldman said. "As principal, I'm going to be going to the game, along with Mr. Roberts as your coach, and now with your mother, we have enough people to transport and supervise."

"My husband is a little jealous that he can't come along," my mother said.

"Will Dad even be back by then?" I asked.

"His business trip is over the next day."

He'd been gone for a whole month. He'd never been gone this long or so far away. Wait...he was in China too...Maybe he'd run into Jerome and Johnnie. No, I was sure it was a pretty big country. Either way, I was really looking forward to him coming back.

The bell rang.

"Well, that's the end of recess," Mr. Waldman said, "and you two should head back to class."

We all got up, and while my mother and Mr. Waldman shook hands, Kia and I exchanged relieved and happy looks. This had all worked out.

"Oh, I had one more question," Mr. Waldman said.

We turned to face him.

"The sod...the letters...that was your *last* surprise, right?"

"Yeah, of course."

"So there's nothing else that might happen that I'm not aware of, correct?"

"Nothing else."

"That's good to hear. Head back to class."

Chapter Nineteen

We pulled up to Greg's house. I went to climb out of the van, but by the time I'd opened the sliding door, he appeared, practically running down the driveway.

"Hey, everybody!" he called out.

He climbed into the backseat to the spot open beside Kia. I was in the middle seat and Lailah was beside me. That was just the way it worked out—it wasn't really my idea. My mother didn't like to have people—kids—sit in what she called the suicide seat, so Kia had climbed into the back when she got in, and then Lailah sat down beside me.

"This is so awesome," Lailah said.

"Yeah, it is," Greg agreed. Then he started chuckling.

"What's so funny?" Kia asked.

"Well, with Nick and Lailah sitting together in the middle seats and you and me back here, it's sort of like we're going on a double date."

"Dream on," Kia said. "The *only* way I'd ever go on any date with you is if...is if...Okay, there's *no* way I'm *ever* going on a date with you."

Everybody laughed. It was sort of a nervous laugh, but I noticed Lailah didn't say anything. That was interesting.

What I was really happy about was that it was my mother driving us instead of my father. Not that there was anything wrong with my father *or* his driving. It was just that he was a lot more likely to say something. Something like asking Lailah how she felt about being my "date," or saying that Kia said no to Greg because she was going to be my wife someday, or saying he didn't want the two girls to fight over me because this wasn't going to be an episode of Jerry Springer or—

"So what do you think?" my mother asked.

Oh great, just what I wanted. I expected this from my father but not my mother.

"Um...I don't think it's such a good idea."

"You don't think it's a good idea that the Raptors could win?"

"What?"

"I was going to ask you if you thought the Raptors could win tonight. What did you think wasn't such a good idea?"

Now I had to think fast. "The way you're going downtown. Dad always goes down the Parkway because it's faster."

"Maybe it is, but it's not nearly as nice a drive."

My hands were sweating. That always happened when I was nervous. I wiped them on my pants. I wondered how that would work if you were holding hands with somebody. Not only would your hand sweat more because you'd be more nervous, but you couldn't very well take it away to wipe it. And it wasn't like she wouldn't notice, because she was holding your hand. Maybe you could hope that she would think it was *her* hand that was sweating.

I risked a little glance at Lailah. She didn't look like the type who would get sweaty hands. She just gave them to other people. She did make me nervous, which, of course, made no sense. I'd spent more time around girls—well, at least *one* girl—than any guy I knew. Kia was always around my house and I was around hers and we played on teams together. Of course Kia wasn't really like a girl. She was more like a guy...or a sister...no, more like a brother. That's what she was—like my brother.

I turned around to look at Kia. I wasn't nervous about looking at her. I thought it was probably best to keep that "like a brother" idea to myself though.

"We're meeting right in the lobby of the Air Canada Centre," my mother said.

"I just hope we're on time," I said.

"We have plenty of time," my mother said.

"I just wouldn't want to miss anything."

"The game doesn't start for another hour and a half," my mother replied.

"That's until the start of the game," I said. "I want to be there for the warm-ups. I want to watch the guys warming up so I can tell how the game is going to go."

"Can you really tell from the warm-ups who will be hot tonight?" my mother asked.

"Of course," I said.

"He's right," Kia agreed.

"That's why you two are such good friends," my mother said. "You've always been like two peas in a pod, which reminds of when you both were little and were in the same—"

"Mom!" I snapped, cutting her off. I knew exactly what she was going to say and I didn't want her to tell anybody that story—not again.

"Okay...I'm sorry. I forgot that you find the story embarrassing."

"It *is* embarrassing," Kia chipped in.

"It's not like I'm going to show anybody the pictures."

She'd done that before too.

"Now I'm curious," Lailah said. "What story?"

"Sorry, I can't," my mother replied.

"Please," she pleaded.

"No story. Actually, you promised you wouldn't tell it again...remember?" I said.

"That's right. I think your father is still planning on showing that picture at your wedding... you know how he always jokes about how you and Kia are going to get married and—"

"Mom, please stop!"

"Wait a second," Greg said. "I remember this story...it's about a bathtub, right?"

"Shut up, Greg," I said.

"And it's a good story," Greg said. "Do you want to hear it, Lailah?"

"I'd *love* to hear it."

"Greg, you should keep your mouth shut," Kia said.

"I didn't promise anybody that I wouldn't tell the story, so it isn't like I'm breaking my word."

"Tell the story and there might be something other than your word that's going to get broken," Kia threatened.

"Okay, okay, I won't tell anybody about you and Nick both being naked and having a bath together."

Kia punched him in the shoulder and he yelped.

"Maybe you should mention that we were six months old at the time," I quickly added.

"Oh, that is *so* cute," Lailah said.

That's just what I wanted, to be thought of as cute.

"I'd love to see that picture," she said.

"Apparently that's only going to happen if you go to his wedding," Greg joked. "So either you have to be invited or you have to marry him."

"No, really," Lailah said. "I just think it's so wonderful that you two have been friends for so long. I don't have *any* friends from that long ago. I've never lived in any house or been to the same school for more than two years."

"That has to be hard," my mother said.

"It is. You're the new kid and you don't know anybody, and everybody else already knows everybody. That first day in a new school is the worst. Walking in and every eye is on you and you just want to be invisible because you know you're being judged."

I remembered her walking in that first day. She looked so confident, like she didn't have a care in the world. I had no idea.

"Everybody already has their friends and little groups, and it's hard to get in."

Kia tapped Lailah on the shoulder and she turned around. "Well, you have friends now," Kia said.

Chapter Twenty

The concourse was alive with people and noise and excitement. There was something about basketball that was like nothing else. We stood right by the Raptors store, waiting for everybody else to arrive. I hated waiting. I just hoped it wouldn't be too much longer.

Kia and Lailah were off to the side by themselves, talking and giggling. Kia wasn't really a giggler, but they did seem to be having fun and—was Kia wearing makeup?

I looked harder. I couldn't be sure—she certainly wasn't wearing as much as Lailah was—but, yes, she did have some stuff on her eyes. I had never seen Kia wear makeup of any sort before. This was bizarre. What was next, press-on nails?

"Hello, everybody!"

It was Mr. Roberts and Mr. Waldman and the rest of the team. Thank goodness, now we could go in. It wasn't like warm-ups were going to wait for us.

"Before we go in, we have one more thing to do," Mr. Roberts said.

I wanted to say, "Let's do whatever it is inside," but I knew that would be rude.

"Do you want to do the honors?" Mr. Roberts asked Mr. Waldman.

"I'm only the principal. You're the coach. I think you should do it."

"Thanks." He turned so he was facing us. "We all know that our school basketball jerseys have seen better days. We also know that, with the decision to change the name of our team to the Raptors in the future, we're going to be getting new uniforms. Well, boys and girls, welcome to the future."

He reached down to a bag at his feet and pulled out a jersey—black and red with *Raptors* in big letters across the front. He held it up and turned it around.

"Number seven...I do believe that's Kia's number."

He handed Kia the jersey. She looked like he'd just handed her a million dollars.

"Are you going to put it on?" Mr. Roberts asked.

"Of course!" She pulled it on over her sweater—that was a really nice sweater she was wearing...Was it new?

One by one he pulled out the jerseys and handed them to the "owner" of that number. With each one I waited for number four to appear, but it was always somebody else's number, until finally I was the only kid not wearing a Clark Raptors jersey.

"I think that's all of them," Mr. Roberts said.

What? What about me?

"Did I forget anybody?" he asked.

Slowly I put up my hand.

"Nick, you didn't get a jersey?"

I shook my head.

"Well, maybe there's one more jersey in here. He reached down into the bag—all the way down into what looked like an empty bag—and pulled out a jersey.

I was so relieved I almost screamed out loud.

On the back of the jersey was my number—a big number 4.

"You know, Nick, maybe that wasn't fair because I did know it was in there. I wanted to save yours for last for a reason. Kia, can you please do the honors for this one?"

She stepped forward and he handed her my jersey. Why would he do that?

"We've been teammates for a long time and a few times we've even been co-captains, like this year. But I asked Mr. Roberts if maybe that could change," Kia said.

"And I agreed," Mr. Roberts said.

She turned the jersey around so I could see the front of it. There was a big *C* at the top.

"You're now *the* captain."

She handed me the jersey.

"I don't know what to say," I stammered.

"Don't say anything, just put it on," Kia said.

I pulled it on over my shirt. I had a terrible feeling that I might actually start to cry—that was no way for a captain to act.

"And," Mr. Waldman said, "in honor of the leadership that Nick has shown, both on and off the court, we've decided that from this point forward our team captain will always wear the number-four jersey as a tribute to Nick."

If I didn't know what to say before, I was completely speechless now.

My mother rescued me by wrapping her arms around me and giving me a big hug. Then Kia gave me a hug as well. Mr. Waldman and the guys all slapped me on the back and shook hands. And then Lailah gave me a hug.

My whole body broke out in a nervous sweat. Thank goodness I had the jersey on top of my shirt or everybody would have seen the sweat pouring off me.

"Now, Clark Raptors, it's time for the game!" Mr. Roberts said to a chorus of cheers and yelling.

We trailed after him, weaving our way through the crowd. He passed by the regular entrance and kept going. That was the way in, but I figured he knew where he was going. Finally our way was blocked by two uniformed security guards seated behind a desk beneath a big sign that said *Corporate Suites*. That's where we were headed.

"Good evening, gentlemen," Mr. Roberts said. "I believe there are passes waiting for us, left by Ms. Allison, for the owners' suite."

One of the men ran his finger down a paper, scanning the list.

"Are you the Clark Raptors?"

As we all stood there in our uniforms, that seemed like a pretty crazy question.

"That's us," Mr. Roberts said.

"We've been expecting you. Please wait and someone will come down to get you," the guard said. He picked up a phone and started talking.

Mr. Waldman had us move over to the side as other people were waiting to get to their private suites.

I watched the people passing by. They didn't look any different than the fans who occupied the regular seats. Well...maybe they were dressed a little better, but why didn't more of them have on Raptors jerseys or hats or T-shirts or something? A lot were dressed up like they were going to some fancy party and not a basketball game.

"Hello, Clark Raptors!"

I looked up. It was Christina Allison—I recognized her from the TV.

She shook hands with Mr. Waldman, Mr. Roberts and my mother.

"And you must be Nick," she said.

"It's nice to meet you, and this is the rest of the team."

I introduced her to each player and she shook everybody's hand.

"It's great to meet all of you. Now let's get upstairs and see the game."

We followed her up a set of stairs and into a corridor—there was carpeting on the floor and pictures of Raptor players on the walls. It certainly was different from the upper deck in the ACC.

"This is it," Christina said.

She opened the door and we filed in. It was really fancy with big comfy chairs, a little kitchen and a gigantic TV screen on one wall.

I walked around the suite with Lailah and Kia, checking everything out, and then went to look down on the court and—

"How about if everybody takes a seat," Christina said.

The team began settling into the big comfy seats that were lined in three rows at the front of the suite.

"Welcome. This luxury box belongs to the team owners, but tonight it's all yours!"

Everybody cheered.

"You can obviously watch the game from the court view seats at the front of the box," she said, gesturing to where I was headed, "or you can also see all the replays up on the Jumbotron or watch the TV broadcast of the game on the big screen on the wall."

I didn't come to the ACC to watch a game on TV.

"And I'm not sure if you're aware, but part of the privilege of being in a private box is that all of your food and drinks are complimentary."

"Complimentary…as in free?" Greg asked.

"As in free."

This time the roar was even louder, partly because I was part of it. I loved basketball and I loved the food that went along with basketball games. This was going to be a wonderful game!

Chapter Twenty-One

Everybody was up on their feet screaming. Not just all of us in the box but everybody in the entire arena. More than nineteen thousand fans were yelling at the top of their lungs, clapping and stomping their feet.

The score was tied at 113, and there were seventeen seconds left in overtime!

"This is incredible!" Kia screamed. "Have you ever seen a game like this before?"

"Has there ever *been* a game like this before?" I yelled back.

The time-out ended and the two teams came out of their respective huddles. It was Boston's ball. Although I wasn't in the Boston huddle and obviously didn't know *exactly* what play they were going to run, I did know what it would involve. Bring it in, be safe, hold the ball until just before the game clock expired and then put up a shot. If they made it, there wouldn't be enough time for the Raptors to get off a play. Either the Celtics would win or they'd have to go to another overtime period.

"Want another dog?" Greg asked.

"What?"

"Another hot dog?" He was holding one in each hand.

"I think I've had enough to eat," I said. "How many hot dogs have you eaten?"

"I lost track after four," he said. "And that's not to mention the pizza and nachos. But what the heck? It is free."

The guys had been eating a lot. Not that I hadn't had my share—two hot dogs, two slices of pizza, and I was working on my third Coke—but I was an amateur compared to some of these guys. For some of them it seemed like eating was far more important than actually watching the basketball game. I didn't come here to eat—even if it was free.

I would rather have been down by the court instead of up here in the box. Not that I wasn't grateful—the owners giving up their private box for us was pretty special—but it still wasn't nearly as good as being courtside or even up in the cheap seats at the top. Up there everybody was a true fan, and nobody came because of the food. It was all about the basketball.

Speaking of which—it was about to begin again. The shot clock was turned off because there only were seventeen seconds left in the game.

The ball came in to the point guard, and the crowd started screaming even louder!

The guard did what was expected. He took the ball up to the top while the other four players headed off into the corners to draw their men away.

He dribbled as the clock ticked down.

Suddenly, off to the side, Wayne left his man and they put a double team on the guard. The guard hadn't seen it coming and was trapped! He tried to find the way out, but they had him so he couldn't get off a pass and—

The ref blew his whistle. He called a foul!

The whole audience groaned and then started screaming!

"That was such a lame call!" Greg yelled through a mouthful of hot dog—little pieces spraying out of his mouth.

"The ref saved him! We had him trapped, we had the steal!" I screamed.

Their guard came to the line.

"What's his free-throw percentage?" Greg asked.

"In the eighties," Kia said.

"Try the *nineties*," I corrected.

"So basically he doesn't miss," Greg said.

"He misses fewer than ten shots out of every hundred free throws he takes," I explained. "He's one of the best free-throw shooters in the NBA."

"And he's six for seven tonight," Lailah added. "And he was perfect from the line *last* game, making all eleven of his shots."

Everybody looked at her, wondering how she knew that.

"It's in the guide," she said, holding it up for us to see. "I love stats."

"Oh...sure."

"So basically we've lost," Greg said.

"Not necessarily. He'll make his shots and we'll still have three point four seconds to get it down for a shot," Kia said. "Right after he shoots, we'll call a time-out and—"

"We don't have any time-outs left," I said. "We used our last one a minute ago."

"We don't even have a twenty-second one?" she asked.

"Nope."

"So...?" Greg asked.

"When he makes the second shot, the clock stops and we have three point four seconds to get it inbounds, all the way downcourt and score."

"That could work to our advantage," Greg said.

"How do you figure that?" I asked.

"The shot will have to be a really long one, way beyond the three-point line. So if we make it we win."

There was some logic to what he was saying. I shrugged.

The fans behind the net started to scream and stomp their feet and frantically waved the little blowups to try to distract the shooter. They were wasting their time and effort. The ball went up and straight in—nothing but net. They were up by one.

"I don't think he's going to miss," I said, more to myself than anybody else.

"Everybody misses sometimes," Kia said.

"I doubt this is going to be one of those times."

He stood at the line, holding the ball in his hands, spinning it slightly, staring at the net. Behind him the fans were all out of their seats, waving and screaming and trying everything they could to distract him. He was so focused he probably didn't even notice them.

Actually it probably would be better for us if he *did* make the basket. If he missed, they'd still be ahead. And they might get the rebound or even scramble it up long enough so we didn't have time to get the ball upcourt and get in a shot. If he scored they were up by two, but we had an inbounds and could at least throw up something and hope for a miracle. But it didn't matter what I hoped for or how the fans were trying to distract him, because he was going to make the shot.

He bent at the knees and put up the shot. Perfect rotation, nice and easy like it was prac- tically hanging in the air, right into the cylinder and—it rimmed out!

The ball went up and bodies crashed together as everybody scrambled for the ball and the ref blew his whistle—somebody was fouled. It was an over-the-back foul on the Celtics! Wayne Dawkins had been fouled just as the clock expired. Both teams were in the penalty, which meant two free throws for us. He'd have to shoot at the line by himself because the game was technically over.

They walked up the court and all the screaming and yelling suddenly stopped. The whole arena was hushed as the referee handed the ball to Wayne for his first shot. He took a breath, bent his knees and took the first shot. It looked good off the release and before I could hold my breath, the ball sailed through the net. Tie game.

Everyone in the arena was on their feet, standing so silently that you could hear a pin drop. The referee handed Wayne the ball again for his last shot—the shot that could win the game! He bounced the ball twice, and the sound echoed throughout the arena.

I leaned out the open window of the suite as far as I could. It was almost like watching the whole thing in slow motion. The ball sailed up into the air, slowly rotating so I could make out the seams. It seemed like everybody in the whole place was holding their breath. It looked like it was heading into the net...no, it was high... it hit the backboard and bounced off the rim and then the backboard and rolled around the rim...and then dropped into the net!

Raptors win, Raptors win, Raptors win!

Chapter Twenty-Two

It took ten minutes for the screaming and cheering to stop and another fifteen minutes before anybody seemed willing to leave their seats and start toward the exits. It was as if it had all been so amazing that nobody wanted it to end. I couldn't blame them. I didn't want to leave. I just wanted to stay there replaying it over and over again.

It was like the Raptors didn't want it to end either. They stayed out on the court long after the buzzer. It looked like there were lots of interviews going on, but I got the feeling that they didn't want the experience to be over. It was because we all had shared in something pretty special—almost magical.

"Can I have all your attention, please!"

We all stopped celebrating and turned to Christina, who was standing at the door.

"That was certainly an incredible game!" she said.

We all cheered out our agreement.

"That was the first overtime win of the season, and you all helped to set your own personal record."

"We did?" Kia asked.

"Yes, we have a final total," she said. She held a little piece of paper in her hands. "The occupants of this suite consumed forty-seven hot dogs, forty-four pieces of pizza, fourteen orders of nachos and forty-two drinks...none of which were beer, thank goodness."

"We ate that much?" Greg asked.

"You practically ate that much yourself," Kia said.

"I contributed, but it was a true team effort," Greg joked.

"And speaking of team," Christina said, "we have a couple more surprises awaiting your team." She smiled. "Surprise number one."

She stepped aside and the door was filled by Jerome and Johnnie Williams!

"What are you two doing here?" I screamed.

They rushed into the suite, all smiles and laughter and high-fiving everybody.

"How's my little sister?" Jerome asked as he picked up Kia, spun her around and then tossed her into the air like she was a rag doll, catching her on the way down! I'd forgotten just how big and strong he was.

"And my teammate...how's it shaking, Nick?" Jerome asked.

"Good, great, wonderful! What are you two doing here?"

"Catching a little bit of basketball. We do like basketball," Johnnie said.

"I meant *here*, in Toronto. You were in Africa, and then you were going to China!"

"We were in Africa—South Africa—spreading the NBA Basketball Without Borders message, and then China and finally Puerto Rico, but the tour ended and we got back quickly because we wanted to be part of the surprise that's been arranged for your entire team."

"A surprise?" I asked.

Both Jerome and Johnnie had gigantic smiles, but neither answered. They turned to Christina.

"Do you want to tell them?" Christina asked.

Jerome shook his head. "You arranged it, so I think you should tell them."

"I appreciate that. You know how everything you've done over the past few weeks has been dedicated to meeting the Raptors." She paused and his smile became even bigger.

This could only mean one thing.

"One of the Raptors is going to come to the school?" Kia questioned.

I hoped it was going to be Wayne Dawkins.

"Even better, you're going to meet *all* of the Raptors!"

The room went wild with people screaming and yelling and slapping each other on the back. The chaos in the room was as long and loud as it had been after the winning basket was scored. Unbelievable, after all that we'd gone through—the letters, emails, getting the whole school to do special projects, changing the name of the team, new jerseys, a Raptors song, and of course the gigantic sod sign—it had worked. We were going to have a school visit from the Raptors—*all* of the Raptors!

"I hope it isn't for a few days," Mr. Waldman said, "so that we have time to give them a royal welcome."

Christina looked at her watch. "Actually you're going to meet them in about fifteen minutes."

"Fifteen minutes...but...but, I don't understand," I stammered.

"You're all going down to the Raptors' locker room to meet the entire team!" Christina yelled, and there was more cheering.

"We have never opened up the locker room to fans like this before, but you're special fans from a special school with some friends in very high places!"

"One in a thousand!" Kia screamed.

"More like one in a million!" Christina added.

This was like a dream come true. Here we were, having watched maybe the greatest game of the season, and now we were heading down to their locker room—the Raptors' locker room— to meet the players! That was incredible...but somehow, something didn't seem right. Maybe it was too fantastic for me to even believe it was real.

"That's amazing!" Greg yelled. "Thank you so much!"

"Okay, everybody, grab your things and let's go and meet the Raptors!" Jerome yelled and everybody cheered.

He led, like the pied piper, toward the door and everybody followed, including my mother and Mr. Waldman and Mr. Roberts.

"Wait until we tell the kids at school," Greg said. "They're not going to believe that we got to meet the Raptors! They're not going to believe it!"

"They are going to be *so* jealous," Lailah said.

Then it came to me what was wrong, why this didn't feel right. I stopped dead in my tracks. *We* were going to meet the Raptors, the twelve of us, but not the rest of the school.

Jerome looked back and saw me standing there, not following behind.

"Come on, Nick!" Jerome yelled as he walked back toward me. "They're going to be waiting."

"I can't go to meet them, JYD," I said.

"What?" he asked.

"I'm not going down to meet the Raptors!" I said loud enough for everybody to hear me over the noise.

Everybody stopped talking and turned to stare at me.

"What did you say?" Kia demanded.

"I'm not going to meet the Raptors."

Now everybody looked confused—no, stunned.

"But...but...why not?" my mother asked.

"Yeah, why not?" Lailah questioned.

This was going to be hard to explain. I gave a little shrug. "It's not that I'm not grateful for you setting this up," I said to Christina. "Thanks for doing it."

"You're welcome...I guess, but I'm confused. This is what you wanted, isn't it?"

I shook my head.

"It isn't?"

"What I wanted was for one of the Raptors to come to the school where *everybody* could meet him, not just me and the basketball team."

"But they might have a chance to meet them next year," Christina said.

"They might, if a Raptor does come, but what about the rest of the grade sixes—our class-mates. They'll be gone next year," I said. "We're here tonight because *all* of those kids helped. And that's why I can't go to the Raptors' locker room."

Everybody looked even more confused.

"Come on, Nicky," Lailah said.

"What if they said that I was the only one who could go into the locker room and nobody else on the team could?" I asked.

"But they didn't say that," Greg chimed in.

"But if they did, would it be fair that only I went and the rest of you had to wait in the hall?" I asked.

"That would suck," Greg said.

"And it wouldn't be fair," I said. "We're a team. So if the whole team couldn't go, I wouldn't want to go either."

"But the whole team *is* going," Lailah said.

"We all get to meet them—everybody," Greg said.

"Not everybody, just everybody on the basketball team," I said. "It wasn't just us that got us here."

"It was just us who made that gigantic sign that got their attention," Greg argued.

"But not just us who sent the letters and the emails and voted to change the school teams' names or did the artwork or—"

"I get the idea," Greg said. "But still...*I* really want to meet them."

"I want to meet them too," Lailah added. "Besides, isn't it better that some of us meet them instead of none of us?"

"It's just...it's just...I can't. If everybody can't meet them, then I can't meet them either."

"What if some of us still want to meet them?" Greg asked.

"I'm not saying *you* can't or shouldn't. I'm just saying I can't go." I turned to my mom. "Do you understand?"

"I guess I do," she said, "although I'm very surprised."

"So am I. How about if we go down to the main entrance and wait for the team until they've met the Raptors?" I said to my mother.

"We can do that," my mother said.

"Okay, everybody...I guess we'll see you all after your visit."

Slowly I walked away, and my mother and I left everybody else behind. It felt like the longest walk of my life with everybody's eyes on me, questioning, wondering if I'd lost my mind. Maybe this wasn't the right decision, maybe I could just turn around and say I'd made a mistake. But no, I hadn't made a mistake. This was the right thing to do.

We walked down the hall and toward the stairs.

"Do you think I'm wrong?" I asked my mother, still questioning my decision, needing reassurance.

"You certainly surprised me...no, *shocked* me."

"But was I wrong?"

"I think you're doing what you think is right."

"You didn't answer the question," I said.

She didn't answer right away, which obviously meant that she *did* think I was wrong.

"Nick, sometimes we all make hard decisions," she said. "This wasn't easy."

"No, and it's getting harder."

"But you did what you believed was right."

"It just wouldn't be right for all of those other kids to work for something that only a few of us get," I said, trying to explain.

"Then, because you thought this through, there's no question that what you did was the right thing," she said.

"Thanks, Mom."

"Sometimes your hardest choices aren't necessarily going to feel so right, right away."

I understood that. It felt *awful*.

"Wait up!"

It was Kia and she was running down the hall toward us. "I'm not going either," she said.

"You don't have to do this," I said.

"I don't have to do anything, but I'm going to do it anyway," she replied.

"You don't think I'm crazy?"

"Oh, no. I *definitely* think you're crazy and probably wrong to toss away an opportunity of a lifetime, but if you're not going, neither am I. Being part of a team is being part of a team."

Suddenly Lailah came running toward us, followed by Greg and what looked like the whole team. Trailing behind them were Mr. Waldman and Mr. Roberts and Christina and Jerome and Johnnie. We waited for them to catch up to us.

"We're all going home," Lailah said. "All of us."

"Really?"

They all nodded their heads in agreement, but they certainly didn't look happy about it.

"Greg?" I asked.

"All of us," he muttered.

"And nobody's mad at me?"

"We're all standing with you," Greg said. "I guess I understand. Maybe I don't agree, but we're a team, right? You're the captain, right?"

I nodded. "Thanks...I appreciate it...but you *really* can go and meet them if you want."

"We're all going home," Mr. Roberts said.

Everybody nodded in agreement.

"Then let's go," Mr. Roberts said.

He shook hands with Christina and then led the group. Kids filed out behind him. All of them had their eyes on the ground. There was no more cheering or smiling or laughing. It felt like we were going to a funeral, and it was all my fault.

I stopped in front of Jerome.

"I'm really sorry," I said. "I know this was a lot of work and you even flew in and I'm sorry."

He bent down and put his hands on my shoulders.

"Don't ever be sorry for doing what you think is right," Jerome said. "Sometimes the easy thing isn't the right thing, and the right thing isn't the easy thing."

"That sounds like something my coach would say."

"You got a smart coach. Now you go home and we'll talk later...Check your email."

Chapter Twenty-Three

It was late when we finally got home. It had been a very quiet car ride from the ACC. It wasn't just that it was like we were driving to—or away from—a funeral, but that I'd been the guy who'd done the killing.

I felt bad. I felt worse than bad. My mother said all the correct things about how what I did was "right," but she was my mother. She was supposed to try to make me feel better. It was, after all, part of her job description.

Even though it was late, I'd hoped that somebody would have called or even emailed to tell me it was okay, but there hadn't been word one from anybody. Then the computer *binged*—I had mail.

I jumped up off my bed, rushed to the computer and then hesitated. Just because somebody was sending me an email didn't mean it was going to be a good email. Maybe somebody was writing to tell me what a jerk I'd been and how I'd lost them a chance of a lifetime. But if I didn't look, I wouldn't know, and it wasn't like not looking was going to change it.

I clicked on my email. One new message—it was from Jerome! That was great...unless *he* was going to tell me that I was wrong.

I looked at the subject line. It read *The Challenge*. I opened the email.

Hey Nick,

I think what you did tonight took a lot of guts. I'm proud of you. The question now is are you ready for a real challenge, to show leadership and help others?

I didn't know what he meant by that. How was I supposed to help anybody? I'm just a kid.

Johnnie and I have been thinking about a project that you and your entire school could team up on to make a huge difference in the world.

You know Johnnie and I were in Africa with the Basketball Without Borders program and I'd mentioned how those kids there love the game but can't even afford shoes to wear. Well, you know Johnnie. He started thinking and decided to call our youngest brother, Joshua, who works at the Basketball Hall of Fame, for some suggestions.

Joshua just emailed us back with the information about an organization that could help put shoes on the feet of those children over there in South Africa and other places.

I want you to visit their website, www.soles-4souls.org, to find out how your team can inspire every student in the school to donate a pair of used shoes to kids like Tulani—that boy I mentioned I'd met in South Africa—who really need them.

I don't usually ask for favors, but I need your help with this and I know you're the type of leader who can make this happen.

JYD

P.S. I hope you enjoyed the game tonight in the owners' suite...and I'm proud of your decision!

There wasn't much question. If Jerome wanted my help, he'd get my help. After all that he'd done for me, I owed him.

Chapter Twenty-Four

The announcements droned on. I wasn't in the mood for them this morning. I just wanted to know if our shoe drive was going to be successful. Today was the day—the day everybody had been asked to bring in a used pair of sports shoes and drop them off at the office before school started. I'd seen some kids with shoes, but we'd been at practice in the gym, so I didn't really know if it would be a whole lot or just a few.

I knew we'd have some shoes because everybody on the team was working on it and we'd all brought in shoes. I was so happy about the team working on this together. Right after the Raptors game I figured some of them—maybe *all* of them—would be mad at me for making them miss the chance to meet the Raptors after the game, but they weren't. They were my teammates, but more importantly they were my friends, and they got behind this project.

●●●

I hadn't slept much the night before. I kept going over everything in my head and hoping we'd be able to gather enough pairs of shoes to make Jerome proud of our efforts—and I guess, more importantly, enough shoes to help those kids in Africa.

"And we have one final announcement," Mr. Waldman said, "concerning our basketball team and its shoe drive."

That got my attention.

"Starting at nine thirty, after we've had time to prepare, there will be a full school assembly about our Clark Raptors and their efforts... I guess you can call it a Raptors assembly. Classes will be called down, grade by grade, starting with the kindergarten classes. And that ends our announcements."

I guess I should have been happy, but I was nervous. I looked around the room. I wondered how many of my classmates had brought in shoes.

"Could everybody please take out a book and read silently until we are called down to the gym," Mrs. Orr said.

Books came out of desks and backpacks around the class. I pulled out my book. I wasn't sure if I was going to be able to concentrate enough to read, but I could open a book.

The kindergarten classes and then the grade-one classes were called down to the gym for the assembly.

I looked over at Kia. She was reading. I tried to catch her eye, but either she didn't see me or she was ignoring me. I waved my hand and—

"Nicholas, do you have a question?" Mrs. Orr asked.

Great, I'd gotten the wrong person's attention.

"No...there was a fly...I was shooing it away."

She didn't look convinced.

The grade twos and the grade threes were called down together. The gym was always filled from the front, with us, the big guys, the grade sixes, at the back. I remembered when *we* used to be the little ones and got to sit up front. That was so long ago. Back then there had been no worries, no problems. Oh, to be young again.

Finally the announcement came for us.

"Line up, please," Mrs. Orr said.

We all lined up at the door.

"You all know my expectations for behavior at the assembly," Mrs. Orr said.

We did. We knew that we weren't just supposed to be well-behaved but were to be the best-behaved kids in the school. She always told us that as grade sixes we had to be role models for everybody else.

She led us down the hall, single file, no talking, to the gym. The gym was already filled and noisy. Judging from the noise level, we didn't have to worry about being the best-behaved. We settled into our section of the floor as the other two grade-six classes did the same.

Mr. Waldman was standing at the front. He raised his hand to signal he wanted silence, and a wave of hands went up and the volume went down to nothing.

"Good morning," he said. "That was excellent assembly behavior. Could we please have the basketball team come forward."

I got up—we all got up—and walked to the front. Half the guys were wearing our new jerseys. I wasn't. Neither was Kia. If we'd known

161

about the assembly, we would all have worn our jerseys. We walked up front, and there on the floor was a gigantic arrangement of shoes. In big, thick letters, three shoes wide—it spelled out *Home Team*! I was stunned!

"We are all so proud of our basketball team," Mr. Waldman said. "Let's give them a big round of applause."

Everybody cheered.

"And while we're proud of what they've accomplished on the court, we're even prouder of what they've done off the court," Mr. Waldman said. "Thanks to their leadership and the efforts of children across the school, we have gathered over five hundred pairs of shoes to be donated to Soles for Souls for children in Africa!"

This time the cheering was even louder. I did feel proud—not just of us, but of everybody who contributed.

"And since today is a Raptors day, I would like to introduce a couple of very special guests who are here to receive the shoes," Mr. Waldman said. "They came here today to say a very special hello. I'd like to introduce a former Raptor, Mr. Jerome Williams, and his brother, Johnnie Williams the Third!"

There was a big cheer as Jerome and Johnnie came through the stage curtain. They gave a big wave to everybody. Then Jerome looked right at me and winked. I knew why they were here—it wasn't just to get the shoes but to make things better for me after what happened at the Raptors game. That was just like Jerome and Johnnie. Maybe the Raptors couldn't come to the school, but one ex-Raptor legend could.

"Hey, Clark Elementary, it's great to be here with you this morning!" Jerome beamed.

"And we're all proud, so proud, of the contributions that you made," Johnnie added.

"That's for sure. You've let us know that it isn't just the NBA that cares, but the students of Clark care," Jerome continued.

"You've shown that anybody, young or old, can make a difference," Johnnie said.

"That you care!" Jerome yelled.

"So when I say 'Who cares?' you say 'Clark cares'...Who cares?" Johnnie yelled out.

We all screamed "Clark cares" as loud as we could, and it was loud!

"Who cares?" Johnnie yelled.

"Clark cares!" we screamed back—so loud the whole gym seemed to shake.

"And finally," Jerome said, "I should introduce some friends of mine who've come to help collect the shoes. Could we please open the curtains!"

The curtain slowly opened to reveal Wayne Dawkins standing on the stage! And beside him was a second Raptor and a third and a fourth and a fifth, and the stage was filled with the entire Raptors team!

I practically fell over!

Jerome and Wayne exchanged a high five, and then Jerome handed him the microphone.

"Good morning, boys and girls of Clark Boulevard Public School!" he called out. "We want to thank our coach for letting us skip practice, and we want to thank you for joining our NBA Cares community team. We really appreciate you letting us drop into your school on such an unscheduled basis. That was very nice of you to be willing to come out of class to meet us."

There was a tremendous round of applause— and was Wayne looking at me?

"How many of you saw our overtime win a couple of weeks ago?" Wayne asked.

Hands and voices were raised across the gym.

"That was a tremendous victory, and the reason we won was because we played as a team. And after our victory we found out how this *whole* school is a team, a team that helps other people, so we had to come out here to meet the entire team."

There was more cheering. One by one each Raptor came up to the microphone to say a few words. Jerome and Johnnie had come off the stage and were standing by the side. Slowly I moved over until I was standing right beside them.

"Thanks for arranging this," I said.

"Wasn't much to arrange. I just let them know what you did, and the whole team insisted on coming out to visit your school."

"Well, thanks for what you did," I said.

"I didn't do much."

I still had one more question I wanted to ask. "When I emailed you to ask about the Raptors coming to the school, you could have arranged it, right?"

He nodded his head. "A couple of them would have come if I asked."

"But you didn't ask them," I said.

"You really didn't ask me to ask them," he said. "Besides, this wasn't about having a Raptor player come and speak."

"It wasn't?" I asked.

"No, this was about *you* getting the Raptors to come, about you not just asking for something for your school, but about you and the school giving something back as well. It wasn't about what *I* could do, but what *you* could do, all of you working as a team to reach your goal— *our* goal—to help others." He paused. "Do you understand?"

"Yeah, I guess I do."

"And you were the leader. Now you better take a minute to figure out what you're going to say."

"Say to who?"

"To everybody. Right after the last Raptor speaks, I'm going to go up, take the microphone and introduce you."

"But what am I going to say?" I gasped.

"Maybe thank the Raptors, maybe thank everybody for helping make this such a success. You'll come up with something."

Jerome gave me a big smile.

I should have been nervous. I should have been terrified. But I wasn't. I would come up with something, and instead of worrying about it, I was just going to enjoy the moment. We'd done it. The Raptors were here.

I smiled, and my smile was almost as big as Jerome's.